BAKER COUNTY
BIGFOOT CHRONICLE
C.G. MOSLEY

SEVERED PRESS
HOBART TASMANIA

BAKER COUNTY BIGFOOT CHRONICLE

Copyright © 2019 C.G. Mosley

WWW.SEVEREDPRESS.COM

ISBN: 978-1-925840-46-9

CHAPTER 1

Tony Joyner and Kurt Bledsoe had been friends since the first time they'd ever met in Mrs. Wilson's kindergarten class many moons ago. Tony had been the shy one, quiet and reserved. Kurt was his polar opposite, rambunctious and mischievous. The two had been inseparable and where you found one, the other was close behind. Not surprising, Kurt's outgoing personality bled over into his confidence level and as it was, he was very sought after by the girls in their high school. With his dark hair, and chiseled good looks, it was no surprise that his girlfriend had been the homecoming queen. June Johnson was blonde, blue-eyed and beautiful—truly a dream girl for all the other boys in the senior class. For this reason, it never made any sense at all to Tony that Kurt frequently cheated on her. He seemed to take her for granted, and although Tony had tried on many occasions to talk sense into him, it was no use. Kurt simply loved girls—even more so than the average teenage boy, Tony thought—and he'd finally come to accept that this trait was just part of who he was.

"Pass me another one," Kurt snapped as he tossed the empty beer can aside.

Tony sighed and shook his head. He already felt his good friend had drunk enough, but it was their last week of school and he could tell Kurt was feeling a bit emotional about the impending end of their childhood and transition into adulthood. Tony could never remember seeing him this down about anything since he'd known him. To make matters worse, he personally looked forward to the drastic change. Tony had been a good student and had many scholarship offers to a lot of the larger schools throughout the southeast. With reluctance, he reached over into the cooler and tossed his friend another ice-cold alcoholic beverage that neither of them had any business drinking.

They were seated in lawn chairs, placed in the bed of Kurt's truck, their backs against the back of the cab. It was a beautiful night with a starry sky that seemed to swallow them up from their secluded spot deep inside the forest. This was a spot that they knew well. It was a safe place to go and discuss their futures and secrets that only the two of them knew. Despite some of his character flaws, there was no one Tony trusted more than Kurt. He himself had always had a crush on June Johnson but she'd never learn from him that Kurt ran around on her. Their friendship was much more important than any girl ever would be.

"There's another one," Kurt said suddenly, pointing up at the sky.

Tony looked up quickly in response but knew it was futile. "Damn—I missed it," he grumbled.

"Gotta keep your eyes open," Kurt replied smugly. "I think I've already seen four and you've only seen one in the hour and a half we've been sitting here."

Tony sighed and took another sip of his own alcoholic beverage (the first and only one he'd had for the night). Truthfully, he *had* been watching the sky and was certain that at least one shooting star had streaked over their heads. With Kurt now on his fifth beer, Tony somehow doubted whether his friend was seeing actual shooting stars or if perhaps his vision was becoming blurry and making him think he was seeing them. It wasn't, however, worth an argument. If Kurt thought he'd seen four, then so be it.

"You decided on a college yet?" Tony asked, glancing over at his friend.

He couldn't make out Kurt's facial features in the darkness, only a dim silhouette but there was no mistaking the uneasiness when the question was asked.

"I told you," he said flatly. "I've got some options but I'm still trying to decide."

Tony breathed deeply through his nose and nodded. He knew that Kurt *said* he'd gotten athletic scholarship offers for his time playing varsity baseball, but he found himself unable to believe it. His gut told him that Kurt had no intentions of going to college and the decision was weighing heavily on him.

"Well whatever you decide, I'm sure you'll be successful at it," Tony said. "You've been good at everything you have done so far."

"That's right," Kurt said, and then he took a long pull from the can. When he finished, he crushed the empty can in his hand and tossed it aside onto the ground beside the truck. Tony shook his head and made a mental note to pick the can up before they left.

"Give me another," Kurt said, belching as he said it.

"No, I think that's enough," Tony said firmly. "You've already drunk way too many to drive so toss me the keys."

Again, Kurt glanced over at him. Tony was unable to see what sort of expression was on his friend's face, but he sensed that it was something bordering annoyance and anger. He braced himself for an argument but to his pleasant surprise, Kurt reached into his pocket, retrieved the keys, and handed them over with no resistance.

"One more shooting star and then we can call it a night," he said, settling back into his lounge chair.

There was a chill in the air and Tony was getting sleepy, but he didn't argue. Though he had no idea how long they'd have to wait before they saw another shooting star, he felt he owed it to Kurt since he'd easily handed over the keys. He relaxed, weaved his fingers behind his head, and kept his eyes focused on the starry mural overhead. Before long, his eyelids grew heavy and soon after that, they closed.

***

"Wake up!" Kurt shouted frantically. "Get up! Did you see that? Holy shit!"

Tony sat up straight and an ominous orange glow to his right gained his immediate attention. "Is that—is that a fire?" he muttered, still trying to figure out if he was awake or still asleep.

"Yes, it's a fire," Kurt said excitedly. He threw his legs off the side of the truck bed and stumbled onto the ground. He moved toward the flames and Tony began to make sense of what he was seeing. Something large had crashed through the forest, leaving a clearly defined path of broken trees and fire in its wake.

"It crashed over there," Kurt said, pointing toward the spot where the flames seemed to begin. "Then it kept crashing and rolling through the trees further down."

The flames weren't large and in fact much of them were beginning to extinguish as Kurt approached.

"Wait," Tony called after him as he clambered out of the truck "What is it? What crashed?"

As crazy as it would've been, Tony fully expected Kurt to respond that a U.F.O. had just crash landed while he'd been asleep.

"Meteor," Kurt answered, still walking between the parallel lines of dying flames that led further into the forest. "I think it was a meteor!"

The irony of what he'd just heard wasn't lost on Tony as he considered the last thing Kurt had said before he'd fallen asleep. *One more shooting star and we'll call it a night...*

"Are you sure we should go over there?" he asked, trying to catch up. "We should probably call somebody?"

Kurt laughed the suggestion off. "We're not calling anyone until we check this out for ourselves first," he replied.

Tony wanted to argue the matter further but knew ultimately his drunken friend would not listen. Initially he was annoyed with the situation and the carelessness Kurt seemed to have regarding the whole thing, but it was short-lived. Tony was also very cognizant of the fact that if he didn't go after him, Kurt could very well injure himself in his inebriated state.

"Wait up," he grumbled as he jogged after him.

The two young men gingerly walked down the hill, careful to avoid embers that remained on the ground all around them. Tony could feel heat creeping up his leg and in his mind's eye he pictured the soles of his shoes melting. They walked on for what he estimated to be at least another sixty yards when suddenly they came upon a large crater in the ground and in the center of it, a large rock with a crack in the middle of it. The odd object almost resembled some sort of galactic egg, Tony thought, but pushed the silly thought aside.

"Wow," Kurt muttered in a voice just above a whisper. "This is badass."

He then began to climb down into the crater.

"Hey, hang on," Tony called after him, but again, it was no use.

Kurt tripped as he stepped over a hedge of dirt and tumbled head over heels. Tony chased after him, concerned that he'd hurt—or possibly burn himself. To his relief, instead of a cry of agony, Kurt began to laugh, an obvious product of his drunken state.

"Are you alright?" Tony called after him. "Get up before you get burned."

"That's the crazy thing," Kurt said over his shoulder as his laughter subsided. "It's not hot—hell, it's cold."

"*Cold?*" Tony asked in disbelief. It was at that moment, he noticed it. The flames that were present only moments before were all but gone now, and as his eyes adjusted, he began to see a strange glow originating from the bottom of the crater. It was blue in color and it began to get brighter with each passing moment. "What the heck is that?" he asked, dumbfounded.

Kurt shook his head as he too began to notice it. The luminescent substance was all over his clothes and hands—an obvious result of the fall he'd had. Overcome with his own sense of disbelief, Kurt placed two fingers on the ground and scooped up a dollop of the strange stuff. He held it up so that Tony could see.

"It's freezing cold—feels like some kind of slime," he said in awe.

Tony looked on as Kurt studied the substance on his fingers, all the while the glow became more intense. Suddenly, with a cadence of panic seemingly coming over him, Kurt began to rapidly thrash his hand wildly as if he was trying to sling the blue goop off his fingers.

"What's wrong?" Tony asked, sensing his panic.

"It's starting to hurt," Kurt replied, his tone worried. "This shit won't come off." Desperate, he then began to wipe the stuff off on his shirt, but to no avail. Whatever it was, it clung tightly to his skin.

"Ow—OWW!" Kurt shouted suddenly, dropping to his knees.

"What?!?" Tony asked, his own voice now stricken with panic. "What is it?"

The blue substance began to spread over the rest of Kurt's hand and continued onward up his arm. It then reached his neck and began to encompass his head. "Oh my god!" he screamed painfully. "Tony! Help me!"

Tony felt his heart rate increase ten-fold but forced himself to stand. "St-stay there," he stammered. "I'm going to get help!"

Without considering the matter any further, Tony ran back to the truck, never looking back. Had he spent just a moment longer surveying the landscape around Kurt, he'd have realized his friend was not the only victim of the strange occurrence in the forest that night.

CHAPTER 2

The wood ape had been watching the two humans for quite some time with a mixture of curiosity and amusement. They'd been seated in the back of the large metal contraption staring at the sky as if they'd never seen the stars before. One of them had been drinking a great deal of liquid from a can and it seemed the more he drank, the stupider he became. The wood ape had seen these two male humans before as this was a spot that the two of them seemed to frequent. He'd lived in the forest with the rest of his tribe for at least twenty winters and, as all wood apes practiced, made sure to keep himself hidden away. He knew that if he was found to have been spotted by a human, it would mean banishment from the rest of the tribe. He'd been warned on more than one occasion by the tribe leader that he was getting too close and becoming careless.

Alas, the warnings he'd been given repeatedly fell on deaf ears. These particular two humans had educated him a great deal, though they had no knowledge that they'd done so. He'd listened in on their many conversations in the forest and had even begun to pick up and understand bits and pieces of their language. He'd picked up, for instance, that most of their conversations revolved around the females of their species. He'd learned that they had names...Tony and Kurt...and a particular female they'd both discussed with regularity was called June.

On this night, one of the male humans—the one called Kurt—seemed upset and almost belligerent about something. The other—Tony—as per usual did his best to encourage his counterpart, but it seemed the more he tried, the more liquid Kurt consumed from the small metal containers he constantly retrieved from the small blue box between them.

The wood ape yawned and glanced up at the stars above, just as the two humans had been doing, though his reason for doing so was quite different. He studied the stars carefully, taking note of their current position as it was his way of getting a good grasp for how late in the night it was getting. It was late enough, he knew, that if he didn't head back to camp the tribe leader would become angry and suspect that he was doing something careless that could endanger them all. He would think this because all members of the tribe were expected to settle in by the mid-point of the night. If a member wasn't there, then others would be forced to look for them. The wood ape knew that if he was found and it was determined that he'd been late because of his infatuation with the two humans he'd been watching, then the consequences for him would be quite severe.

With a bit of reluctance, the wood ape turned and began the trek down the hill that would lead him back to the camp. He hadn't walked far when suddenly a bright light enveloped him from somewhere behind. He'd had only a brief moment to turn and see what appeared to be a ball of fire hurtling toward him. Using his powerful legs to propel himself forward, the wood ape moved swiftly further down the hillside and just as the ball of fire bore down upon him, he managed to roll out of the way. The impact, however, created a bit of an explosion that hurtled the large beast through the air, causing him to crash painfully against a tree. The collision with the tree in turn threw him right back toward the object that had just crashed into the soil. He then determined that the object was actually some sort of large boulder.

The wood ape was bleeding profusely from an injury to his head, and then felt something cool enveloping his legs. He clumsily climbed from the crater and rolled to the earth on the other side, frantically trying to put distance between himself and the strange rock. When he finally rested at the base of a tree, the wood ape noticed a strange glowing substance covering the lower half of his body. He quickly determined that, whatever the substance was, it had evidently come from the large rock. A sensation of panic began to set in and the wood ape began to try to remove the glowing substance from his lower appendages. He tried to use dirt as a means to remove it and when that didn't work, he used a pinecone. Neither seemed to do any good and the wood ape soon came to realize he had a new problem.

The two humans had climbed down the hill to investigate as they too had apparently noticed the burning rock. For the briefest moment the wood ape wondered if they'd spotted him too, but their attention seemed to be fully on the rock. This was a relief to him, but he was cognizant of the fact that if he was to remain unseen, his skills of stealth that all wood apes possessed would be put to the ultimate test. He'd never been so close to humans before. The wood ape was so close he could smell them, and he wondered if they could smell him too.

As he watched the one called Kurt climb into the crater, he began to feel an odd sensation on his legs. The glowing substance began to somehow bore its way through the thick hair and ultimately penetrate his skin. The pain was intense, and it was all the wood ape could do not to howl. As the large beast struggled to keep his composure, he suddenly noticed that Kurt had gotten the substance on his own appendages and he too was evidently beginning to feel a similar pain. The human however, made no attempt to hide the torment he was now feeling. Kurt began to scream.

The other human—Tony, seemed concerned and frightened all at once. He tried to mutter something comforting to Kurt, but the tormented human continued to scream and thrash on the ground. The wood ape then noticed that the glowing substance began to cover more and more of the human's body, until finally his entire arm and neck was enveloped. Tony turned and fled. It was then that the wood ape noticed that he too was becoming covered by more of the strange glowing substance. It moved up his legs and then began to constrict his waist.

With Tony now gone, and the other human seemingly drawing his last breaths, the wood ape could no longer fight off the urge to howl in pain. It did so, and it moved back toward the crater, finally collapsing beside the human. The wood ape caught a glimpse of the human looking at him, his eyes filled with fear and amazement. However, the screaming continued and the two of them—species that were never meant to mingle - thrashed and rolled wildly on the ground as the glowing substance soon consumed their entire bodies.

CHAPTER 3

The middle of the night in Dunn, Mississippi, was much like you'd expect in any other small town located in America. The streets were for the most part barren and almost every business was closed for the night, save the two gas stations that bookended the town limits. Probably the liveliest spectacle to be found in the dead of night was the lone traffic light in the town square that blinked red until 7 a.m. the next morning.

Sheriff Ray Cochran, a burly mammoth of a man in his mid-fifties, pulled up to that very traffic light and killed the engine of his patrol car. He wasn't sure what he was looking for, but he'd sent his deputy home for the night and decided that he'd spend an hour or so in the middle of town to keep an eye out for drunks and speeders. It was a Friday night in early November and with the Baker County Bearcat football season in the books, the young folks in town had little else to do besides drive down every country road in the county. And as bored young people ventured out on their own into the night, it was never a shock to Cochran when he occasionally caught them partaking in the use of alcohol. He'd noticed the problem getting worse in recent years and he was unable to put his finger on exactly why. He wondered if perhaps the parents of today's kids cared less than they did when he was that age. As he considered that possibility, he quickly pushed the thought aside, refusing to accept such a horrendous explanation. It was much more likely that the parents of the late '80s were simply busier. Just about every pair of parents he knew in Baker County both worked—a stark difference in how things worked when he was younger. The days of the man being the breadwinner and the woman being the homemaker were apparently over.

As his mind began to wander further into the rabbit hole of what constituted good parents in 1988, he began to stare at the blinking red traffic light. He'd become entranced and felt his eyelids begin to get heavy. Just as he was beginning to succumb to exhaustion, the roar of an approaching automobile startled him back to life. It was a beat-up blue Ford F-150 and he immediately recognized it as the one belonging to Kurt Bledsoe. Kurt wasn't what Cochran would call a "bad kid", but he knew him well enough to know he was exactly the kind of young man he'd just been thinking about. The high rate of speed and the jerky movements of the vehicle all indicated a strong possibility that he had indeed been drinking alcohol.

Sheriff Cochran cranked the car, its engine roaring to life, and chirped the tires as the massive vehicle lurched forward, the blue strobes on the roof swirling all at once. The driver of the blue truck, presumably Kurt Bledsoe, noticed him immediately and slammed on the brakes. Cochran angled the patrol car in front of him, the Baker County courthouse looming large over them. The door on the truck swung open and the sheriff was surprised to see that it wasn't Kurt Bledose after all, though he was certain that it was his truck.

"Sheriff! Sheriff!" the young man screamed as he ran toward Cochran.

Cochran was standing behind the open driver's door of his patrol car. The aggressive nature in which the teenage boy was coming at him took him off guard and he instinctively reached for his sidearm.

"I need your help! In the forest—please come to the forest!"

"Tony Joyner?" Cochran asked, squinting. "Is that you?"

"Yessir," the boy replied frantically. "Kurt is in the forest and he's hurt—I tried to help but..."

"Get in the car," Cochran commanded as he himself climbed back behind the steering wheel.

Tony got in and the sheriff immediately righted the car and turned on the sirens. The large boxy car had a powerful engine, so much so that Tony felt himself sink into the faux leather seat as they accelerated past the "LEAVING DUNN" sign at the north edge of town.

"What the hell were y'all doing out in the forest this time of the night?" Cochran asked.

Tony looked away sheepishly. "I don't know...just talking," he mumbled. Suddenly, he whipped his head back to look at the sheriff as his thoughts returned to his ailing friend. "We've got to hurry—something got him...it came from the meteor."

Sheriff Cochran glanced at Tony curiously. "Meteor?" he asked with a raised eyebrow. "What do you mean *something* got him?"

"I mean...I guess it was a meteor," Tony replied shaking his head. It was as if there were a million thoughts scrambling around in his head and he was trying to put them back in order. "It was a big rock...it had a crack in it and...this stuff, it was coming out and it got on him. It was hurting him."

Cochran could clearly tell that Tony was not intoxicated but he could smell the faint aroma of alcohol. "Son, I've got to ask...were y'all drinking out there?"

Tony bit his lower lip and rubbed his hands over the brown hair atop his head. He seemed incredibly bothered by the question and his posture provided the response Cochran needed.

"Relax," he said calmly. "We'll get him."

Once they finally arrived at the parking area next to the playground, Tony pointed to the horse trail that led into the forest. Cochran looked at the trail and then back to Tony, an expression of disapproval on his face.

"Trucks aren't allowed on those trails," he muttered.

"Yessir, I know," Tony said. "But we knew no one would be out there this time of the night."

Cochran sighed. "Will my patrol car make it down there?"

Tony considered the question and then nodded. "Yessir, it's plenty dry enough and it's mostly gravel."

With a bit of caution, Cochran eased the wide car onto the trail and though it initially seemed too narrow, it eventually widened out to the point where he felt comfortable enough to drive a little faster. He estimated the drive to where Tony and Kurt had been parked took almost ten minutes—a surprisingly long way for them to be into the forest at that time of the night. The sheriff and many locals knew of tales regarding the presence of a tribe of bigfoots that lived in the forests of Baker County. Many dismissed the tales as nothing more than local folklore, but Sheriff Cochran knew better. He'd seen the legendary wood ape with his own eyes and knew that it was very much a real creature. Of course, not everyone would be convinced, and he was okay with that—as a matter of fact he preferred it. The less the public knew about them, the better. He felt certain that Kurt and Tony must not have put a lot of stock into the tales that they'd undoubtedly heard at some point during their lives in Dunn. Had they truly believed, he was certain that they would've never ventured so far into the forest at that time of the night with the knowledge that the wood apes were out there watching them.

"Right there!" Tony said suddenly, and he pointed. "We were parked right there!"

Sheriff Cochran brought the car to a halt and snatched up his flashlight as he exited the vehicle. As soon as it flickered to life, he scanned the beam of light over the surrounding landscape and settled it on something small, white and cylindrical resting on the ground.

"That yours?" he asked, keeping the light steady on the beer can.

Tony immediately thought back to the can Kurt had thrown out of the truck. The one he'd made a mental note to pick up before they left. "Kurt threw it down," he said. "I was going to pick it up—but then…"

"The meteor," Cochran interrupted as he glanced up at the twinkling stars above them. He continued to survey the surroundings when he spotted an odd trail of burnt grass and splintered trees of all sizes down the hillside ahead of them.

"That's where it came down," Tony explained. "I left Kurt down there."

"Okay," Cochran said, pulling his sidearm with his free hand. "Stay behind me, and if I tell you to run, you get your ass back to the car and you don't look back…got it?"

"Yessir," Tony replied.

They moved down the hill and into the blackness below. The only sounds to be heard were that of an owl and the occasional yip of a coyote. Otherwise it was deadly silent. Just as Tony mentioned that they were almost there, Cochran noticed the ominous silhouette of what appeared to be a large boulder ahead of them.

"What the—"

"That's it…that's the meteor," Tony stammered.

Sheriff Cochran directed the beam of light onto the rock and could see the large crack that had formed in its center, just as Tony had described, however he didn't see any sort of *stuff* coming out of it.

"You said something was coming out of the rock?"

"Y-yeah," Tony said, and he stopped where he was, seemingly afraid to get any closer. "It was some gooey slime looking shit—it was glowing blue."

"Well I don't see anything glowing blue," Sheriff Cochran mentioned with a bit of skepticism.

Cautiously, he made his way around the rock, his gun still drawn and pointed ahead of him. "Kurt Bledsoe—you out here son?"

There was no response.

Cochran surveyed his surroundings carefully and as the beam from his flashlight washed over the soil ahead of him, he spotted something troubling. There were footprints all over the ground— but they clearly were not human. They were large, nearly two feet in length. They were clearly put there by a wood ape.

As far as Cochran knew, the bigfoot tribe that lived in Baker County had never harmed a human being and based on his own personal experiences, they did everything they could to stay hidden away and as far from humans as they could get. However, even knowing all that, he couldn't help but feel a sinking feeling come over him. The notion that a wood ape could've snatched up an incapacitated Kurt Bledsoe and dragged him off into the middle of the night never to be seen again was a troubling thought, but at the same time a logical one under the current circumstances.

"Kurt!" Tony called out from behind him. "You out there man? I've got the sheriff here!"

Still there was silence.

"You don't see him?" Tony asked Sheriff Cochran.

"No," he muttered in reply. "I don't. Head back to the car, I'm going to venture a little further down. I'll be back soon."

Tony said nothing but did as he was told and jogged back to the patrol car. Meanwhile, Sheriff Cochran walked onward, keeping his head on a swivel. There was tension in the air. It was thick and hot and signaled something bad was near. To the best of his recollection, Cochran thought there was a stream directly ahead. He decided he'd walk as far as that stream and if he still saw no sign of Kurt, he'd head back to the car and request back up. A few more minutes of walking among majestic pines that reached for the stars and finally the bubbling of water signaled that he'd reached his intended destination.

Sheriff Cochran again shined his flashlight around the surrounding landscape. Suddenly, a flash of white came into view and he immediately recognized it to be a shoe. Cochran jogged over to it and knelt to examine the footwear without touching it. He looked closely for any blood, or even the glowing blue substance that Tony had mentioned. He saw nothing.

"Kurt Bledose? You out here?" he asked, glancing all around him.

A cool breeze rolled off the stream that made him shudder. He pulled the top of his jacket together tightly and resisted the urge to tremble. As he stood back up, his knees popped and then they popped again…only the second time he realized it wasn't his knee that made the sound. It was the twigs on the ground behind him. He spun around sharply, the gun and flashlight moving with him to see who—or what—was sneaking up behind him.

"What in the literal hell?" he asked with a mixture of shock and bewilderment.

Standing before him was Kurt Bledsoe. His eyes were open and at first, he appeared to be looking at the sheriff, but as Cochran studied him closer it became more apparent that he was actually looking *through* him instead. It was almost as if he had no idea he was there at all.

"Are you alright, son?" he asked softly.

No response.

"What happened to you?"

Still nothing.

The sheriff shook his head and began to unzip his large coat. He then moved toward Kurt, who still didn't seem to acknowledge his presence, and draped the jacket over his shoulders. As if the situation was not already odd enough, it had suddenly become even more curious because for reasons that Cochran could not come to terms with at the time, Kurt Bledsoe was completely naked.

CHAPTER 4

The Baker County Hospital was located on the outskirts of the town of Dunn. Sheriff Cochran took Kurt Bledsoe straight there for observation. He and Tony had made multiple attempts to get the young man to talk, but he would not respond. Kurt would instead stare blankly out the window of the patrol car: clearly his mind was somewhere else. With regards to his lack of clothing, Tony was just as dumbfounded as the sheriff and could offer no explanation.

When they arrived at the hospital, Tony jumped out of the passenger seat and opened the rear car door to make one more attempt to get through to Kurt. He knelt in front of him and looked up into his friend's eyes.

"Kurt, what the hell happened out there?" he asked, almost pleading.

Kurt stared past him toward the forest behind the hospital.

"Did something get you after I left?" Tony asked.

For the first time, Kurt's gaze slowly lowered to meet Tony's. He said nothing, but Tony saw something in his friend's eyes that he'd never seen before. Fear was there, but there was much more than that. Confusion, sadness, despair...it was all there in a collection of unbridled emotions that had seemingly overwhelmed Kurt's brain.

"Okay, Tony," Sheriff Cochran said, gently pulling him aside. "Let's get him inside."

Tony looked over his shoulder and found a male nurse standing there patiently, a wheelchair in front of him.

"We'll take good care of your friend," he said as he stepped forward. Another man joined him and a moment later they were wheeling him through sliding glass doors.

Sheriff Cochran and Tony followed and once they were inside, Tony was directed to have a seat in the waiting area. The sheriff spoke to two other hospital employees for at least half an hour before returning. He glanced at his watch as he had a seat next to Tony.

"You need to call your mother," Cochran said. "It's three in the morning—she must be worried sick about you."

Tony shook his head. "Mom works nights at the box factory," he replied. "As far as she knows, I'm at home asleep."

Sheriff Cochran shook his head with disappointment but resisted the urge to lecture. "Okay," he said. "Well you still need to let her know what's going on."

Tony took a deep breath and then slowly looked over at the sheriff. "I'd rather not," he said softly.

Cochran smiled and shook his head, this time in disbelief. "Son, if you don't tell her, I'm going to tell her." He paused and pointed toward the desk he'd just walked away from. "Go over to that desk, ask to use the phone, and call your mother. Let her know what's going on and that you're with me."

Tony looked over at the desk and sighed. "Alright," he said, sounding defeated. "I'll call."

"Attaboy," Cochran replied.

Once Tony was away with the phone against his ear, Sheriff Cochran quietly stood and made his way through a pair of swinging wooden doors that led to the observation rooms. He stopped at the nurses' station and asked where to find Kurt Bledsoe. She told him room six and a few seconds later he arrived just as the doctor was walking out.

"What's wrong with him, Dr. White?" Cochran asked as he and the doctor made eye contact.

The doctor took a deep breath through his nose and removed his glasses. He looked exhausted—or maybe it was unnerved. "I'm not sure," he muttered. "His adrenaline levels are through the roof. They are so high in fact that he should be dead."

Cochran's eyes widened. "What? Dead?"

Dr. White nodded. "Too much adrenaline can cause damage to the heart. It's as if his flight or fight response kicked in but still hasn't stopped yet. It doesn't make any sense."

"Would that cause him to act the way he's acting? So...distant?"

The doctor considered the question. "Well, I think he's clearly suffering from shock, but his strange behavior goes beyond that. I need to know more about what happened out there."

Sheriff Cochran breathed deeply, his large shoulders moving slightly. "I've given you all the information I have. Frankly, I think a lot of that business about glowing goop coming out of the rock was a bunch of B.S. What we have here are two teenagers that went out in those woods and drank themselves silly. Imaginations went wild."

"What that boy is suffering from is not a result of his imagination, Sheriff," the doctor said. "He's also suffering from a fever which as you may know is the result of the body trying to fight some sort of sickness or trauma."

Cochran's brow furrowed with curiosity. "What are you saying, doc?"

Dr. White's eyes narrowed, and he looked around to see if anyone was listening. "Have you notified the boy's parents of what is going on?"

Cochran shifted uneasily. "His mother died...his father has been long gone. He lives with his sister and no I haven't contacted her yet."

Dr. White nodded. "Good, that'll give us a bit of time." He closed his eyes as if he were planning something out in his head. "Sheriff, we need to take the boy to the Walker Laboratory for further evaluation."

Sheriff Cochran was taken aback. He cocked his head and asked, "What the hell for? What can they do that you can't do?"

Again Dr. White looked uncomfortable and looked around. "They have equipment there that I don't have here. Whatever is wrong with him is unlike anything I've ever seen before. I want to transport him there and *then* you let his sister know where he is at."

Sheriff Cochran sighed and ran his fingers through his salt and pepper hair as he considered what Dr. White had just said. Walker Laboratory was a mystery to most people in the town. Cochran knew that the federal government funded the facility, but little was known about what they actually did there. He'd been in the front lobby of the building before, but never had the opportunity to venture in any further. There were some in town that speculated the lab had something to do with aliens or U.F.O.'s. This particular rumor currently troubled him as he considered the strange circumstances surrounding the rock that had fallen from space. As otherworldly thoughts began to creep throughout his mind, Cochran shook his head to regain his composure.

"Doc, I know you're the expert and all, but can you give me a little more to go on here?" Cochran asked nervously. "This kid seems messed up in the head, but I don't really see anything physical going on."

"The neurological problems that he's having right now are…complicated," Dr. White said cryptically. "Trust me, we need to get him looked at with the equipment over at Walker."

Again, Sheriff Cochran sighed. "Alright, hurry up though 'cause I'm about to call the sister."

Dr. White nodded and disappeared through a door that Cochran could only assume led to Kurt Bledsoe. He returned to the lobby where Tony Joyner was waiting. His face was ashen, and it seemed obvious that the conversation he'd just had with his mother had not gone well.

"My mom is on the way to get me," he said somewhat bitterly. "She was pretty pissed."

Cochran smirked at him. "I'm not surprised," he said, amused. "How's Kurt?"

The sheriff shifted his large frame from one foot to the other. "He's okay for the most part," he said. "They're gonna take him over to Walker Laboratory for further evaluation."

Tony scratched his head and squinted. "Evaluation for *what*?" he asked. "They think Kurt's got some kind of alien virus or something?"

Sheriff Cochran shook his head quickly. "No, of course not," he grumbled. "And don't you go around telling folks that either."

Tony looked away. "Alright," he replied, realizing he'd said something wrong. "Don't worry, I'll keep my mouth shut."

Cochran eyed him and somehow doubted that Tony would indeed keep quiet. He was just about to press him on the matter when a red sedan came to a furious stop just beyond the sliding glass doors. A brunette woman, early forties, jumped out of the car and stormed through the glass doors.

"Tony, what the hell?" she spat angrily. She then glanced at the sheriff and offered a polite   smile. "Thanks for seeing after him Sheriff," she said almost as an afterthought.

"It was no problem," he answered. "Good kid—just got involved in a bit of stupidity tonight. I see it all the time."

She nodded and forced a smile to hide the anger she was feeling toward her son. "I bet you do," she muttered. "Well, I'm gonna get him home. Thanks again!"

Sheriff Cochran crossed his arms. Tony glanced back over his shoulder at him and the sheriff nodded and smirked in response.

One down, one to go, he thought. Cochran ventured back outside into the cool night air and as he reached for the car door handle, he noticed an ambulance pulling away at the far side of the building. He snatched up the radio mic and called Shelly, the Baker County dispatcher who was, to the best of his knowledge, the only other member of the sheriff's department currently on duty. The radio crackled to life.

"How can I help Sheriff?"

"Shelly, I need an address for Marie Bledsoe...used to be Connie Bledsoe. I think they live somewhere near the water tower on the other end of town."

"Stand by," Shelly replied all business-like.

After a few moments of silence, the radio crackled to life again. "The address I have for Connie Bledsoe is 197 Blue Ridge Rd...does that sound right?"

"That's it," Cochran replied as he started the car. "I'm headed over there to retrieve Marie. Her younger brother has been injured so I'm gonna take her to him."

"10-4," Shelly answered and again the radio fell silent.

CHAPTER 5

Marie Bledsoe was known throughout Dunn for two things: First she was a beautiful woman, and secondly, she was a hell of a good mechanic. She'd had a few long-term relationships with men throughout the years, but her biggest and most steady love seemed to be with the automobile. No one in town was better when it came to diagnosing and fixing an ailing car. Marie was in her late twenties and had dark hair that fell just above her shoulders, gorgeous green eyes that always seemed to sparkle, and one couldn't help but notice the shiny assortment of studs, diamonds and other trinkets that decorated her ears. She was stunning to look at but could be a major force to reckon with if angered.

Sheriff Ray Cochran brought the boxy patrol car to a halt at the curb, just in front of the bright red mailbox with BLEDSOE scrawled across it in black lettering. When he stepped out, to the east he was beginning to see the slightest hint of sunrise, evidenced by a subtle hue of purple that began to overtake the black. He stepped onto the driveway and immediately noticed the garage door was open and the light was on inside. It was then he caught sight of a pair of denim covered legs protruding from underneath the driver's side of an old sky-blue Chevy Chevelle, each foot encased in a heavy brown boot.

"Who's out there?" a female voice called from underneath the car. "Don't screw around with me, I'm always armed!"

Cochran smiled and placed both his hands on his hips. "Marie Bledsoe? This is Sheriff Ray Cochran…would you mind coming out for a second? I need to talk to you."

Without hesitation, the body under the car rolled out into the open. Cochran looked down at the grease-smudged pretty face and immediately noticed her concerned expression.

"Is this about Kurt?" she asked, sitting up.

"Yes, it is," Cochran said, offering a hand to pull her up. She took it and dusted her pants off.

"What's wrong with him?" she asked, sounding almost as if she didn't really want to hear the answer. "I've been out here waiting on him to get home all night. I was gonna give him a real talking to—"

"He's okay," Cochran said, gently interrupting. "He got into something out in the forest and he's being checked out. I came by to take you to him."

She nodded. "Alright, well thank God he's okay," she said, obvious relief in her tone. She reached into the car and grabbed a jacket. "He won't be okay when I get through with his ass, let's go."

Cochran followed her back to the car and resisted the urge to ask if she wanted something to wipe the grease smudges from her face. Had it been any other woman, he'd have thought more of it, but Marie Bledsoe couldn't care less.

As the car rumbled along the highway, she asked, "Sheriff what exactly did my brother get into?"

Cochran took a deep breath and exhaled slowly. "Well," he replied. "Marie, it's pretty crazy and I'm not sure if I'm the one to tell you. Maybe you should wait and ask your brother."

She glared over at him, skepticism in her eyes. "Tell me Sheriff," she said. "What happened to my brother?"

"Alright," he said, clearing his throat. "Here goes. Your brother was in the forest with Tony Joyner...you know him?"

Marie nodded. "He's Kurt's best friend, of course I know him."

"Okay, well they were out there drinking," he said, pausing to glance over at her.

Her mouth became a tight line and her eyes narrowed. "Go on," she urged.

"Well, Tony told me that a meteor came down and struck the ground near them. Your brother took off to investigate and—this is where it gets crazy—Tony says something was leaking from the meteor and Kurt got whatever it was on his skin. It...did something to him...he's not himself."

"What do you mean he's not himself?" she asked, arching an eyebrow.

He gripped the steering wheel tightly. "Well, he's not really talking to anyone. He's not really looking at anyone. He seems fine physically but mentally something else is going on."

Marie slowly turned her head away and looked out the passenger window. She said nothing for a long moment and just watched the pine trees zip past. Finally, she said, "You're right, that does sound crazy."

"I told you."

"But if Tony Joyner said that was what happened, then I assure you that is what happened," she added. "He's a trustworthy kid and if it weren't for him Kurt would probably stay in trouble all the time." She looked back over at the sheriff. "Are they gonna be able to help him?"

He sighed. "I'm not a doctor, Marie, but I'm confident that they will."

The car rumbled along for a long while and as they passed by the entrance to the hospital, Marie shifted uneasily in the passenger seat. "Wait," she said, a hint of panic in her voice. "The hospital...you just..."

"Yeah," Cochran replied. "Your brother isn't at the hospital."

Marie turned her whole body to look at him, but before she could speak, he added, "I mean, he *was* at the hospital, but the doc took a look at him and thought he needed some other tests done over at the Walker Laboratory."

"Walker Laboratory?" Marie asked, obviously dumbfounded. "I've never heard of anyone going there to get medical treatment. I thought that was some place where they do research on aliens—like an Area 51 kinda place."

Cochran laughed nervously. "Nah, there's nothing to that," he said, knowing full well he had no idea what it was they did there. "Whatever you've heard is all rumor."

"Okay," she said, pausing to purse her lips as she thought, and then: "Have you ever heard of anyone receiving medical treatment there?"

The sheriff forced a smile and nodded. "Sure, it's happened before," he lied.

When they arrived at Walker Laboratory, Cochran brought the big patrol car to a halt next to the guard shack. Beyond the striped barrier (which was nothing more than a painted board that could mechanically lift up and down), a large gray structure loomed at the end of the long dark driveway. The building was three stories in height with each floor adorned with rows of mirrored glass windows. The roof was peppered with antennas and satellite dishes of various sizes.

"Evening, Sheriff," the slender guard said as he tossed a newspaper he'd been reading aside. He was older, probably early sixties, and looked bored out of his mind. His hair was silver, and almost as an afterthought, he reached over and put on a hat that completed his uniform.

Sheriff Cochran glanced up at the eastern sky that was becoming brighter by the minute. "I think good morning is probably more appropriate at this hour," he replied.

The guard leaned out of the shack where he could get a good look. "Ah, so it is," he said with a chuckle. He glanced back at the sheriff and his eyes moved past him to where Marie was sitting, staring at him intensely. "How can I help you this morning?"

"Baker County just sent an ambulance over here a little while ago," Cochran replied. "There was a teenage boy transferred here. I'm coming to check up on him."

The old guard nodded, but he kept watching Marie with obvious curiosity.

"This is his sister," Cochran added. "As you can imagine, she's concerned and wants to see him."

There was a flash of a smile and another nod. "Oh yes, of course," the guard muttered, and he reached for a button just inside the door that raised the barrier so they could pass. "I'll alert the front desk that you're coming."

"Much obliged," the sheriff muttered as the big car eased forward.

"Why does this feel like an episode of *The Twilight Zone*?" Marie asked as she stared at the ominous building.

Though Sheriff Cochran knew what she meant—he could feel it too. There was tension in the air and it was thick and intimidating. There was a row of parking places along the front of the building—most of which were unoccupied. Cochran figured it was because of the time of day, but as most of the spaces were marked for doctors and other laboratory staff, he still had to park at the furthest end of the row. No sooner had he put the car in park did Marie bolt out of the car.

"Hang on," he called after her, quickly slamming his car door.

She either didn't hear him, or chose not to hear him, because Marie jogged to the glass door entrance that led to the lobby.

"Where is Kurt Bledsoe?" she barked at a surprised guard that was sitting behind a massive black desk against the wall.

He stood and moved his right hand closer to his sidearm. "Excuse me?" he asked. "Who are you?"

Sheriff Cochran stormed in and gently grabbed Marie by the arm. "We're here for the Bledsoe kid," he explained. "This is his sister...the guard out there said he'd let you know we were coming."

The guard's hand moved away from his weapon and the lines of his face softened. "I see," he muttered as he stepped back to the desk. "Didn't get the message...I was away taking a leak." He then picked up a phone and muttered only two words to whoever was on the other end.

"They're here."

A moment later, he hung up the receiver and pressed a button on the wall beside the desk. "Through those doors," he said, pointing to two black doors that opened across from where they were standing.

Sheriff Cochran nodded his thanks and he and Marie briskly moved through the opening. They found themselves standing in a long hallway. There was white tile on the floors, sheetrock walls painted beige, and white fluorescent lighting set into the drop ceiling above. There were numerous wooden doors along the walls and near the end and to the right, a man in a white lab coat stood, watching them.

"This way," he called to them, motioning for them to approach.

"Is my brother alright?" Marie called out worriedly.

"Your brother is back here," the man answered, gesturing toward the open doorway beside him.

Marie's pace quickened, and Sheriff Cochran jogged to keep up.

When they finally made it to where the man was standing, he held out his hand to Marie. She in turn ignored it and peered into the room. Kurt was lying on a hospital bed with no less than four nurses standing around him, all of them wearing surgical masks over their faces. There were multiple machines surrounding him too, one of which seemed to be recording his heart rate and blood pressure on a digital screen.

"What's wrong with him?" she asked, approaching.

The man grabbed her by the arm. "Wait," he said. "Keep your distance…we're still trying to determine what's wrong with him."

Marie wrenched her arm free. "I want to speak to him," she snapped. "You're not going to keep me from speaking to my brother." She looked at Cochran, her green eyes pleading with him to back her up.

"I'm sorry, we haven't been introduced," the sheriff said, holding out a hand to the man. "I'm Ray Cochran."

The man nodded and smiled, his lips parted revealing strikingly white teeth, all straight. "Of course, Sheriff," he replied, shaking his hand. "I'm Doctor Franklin."

"So, what's the story with the kid?" Cochran asked. "And what do we need to do to get Marie close enough to talk to him?"

Doctor Franklin bit his lip and looked at Marie. His gaze slowly moved to Kurt, lying motionless in the hospital bed. "Well," he said, his mind wandering, "I suppose it may do him good to hear from his sister."

"Of course, it would," she said, taking a step forward.

Dr. Franklin grabbed her arm again. "But, you need to take precautions," he said quickly. He looked toward the nurse nearest him. "Take her down the hall and get her into a mask, gloves and gown," he said. He paused and looked at the grease smudges on her face. "And wash her hands and face."

The nurse nodded and beckoned Marie to follow. She glanced at Cochran, who smiled to reassure her. "I'll be right here finding out what I can," he said.

She nodded and followed the nurse out of the room, eventually disappearing further down the hallway.

"What kind of tests are you running on him?" Cochran asked when he was certain Marie was out of earshot.

Dr. Franklin had a thick head of brown hair which he was now running his fingers through. The gesture seemed to be a product of nervousness. Something about Franklin seemed off. He looked to be mid-thirties, tall and slim. There was quite a bit of stubble on his face and the dark circles under his eyes suggested exhaustion.

The doctor sighed and said, "Sheriff, I'm not really at liberty to say at the moment."

Sheriff Cochran shifted his weight from one foot to the other and placed both his hands on his hips. His brown eyes narrowed as he stared hard into Franklin's hazel ones.

Doctor Franklin, clearly sensing Cochran's building frustration, quickly said, "Sheriff, you know we are a federally funded operation and a lot of what we do here is top secret. I could be thrown in prison for saying something I legally am not allowed to say."

Cochran shook his head. "Don't give me that government bullshit," he spat. "Tell me what the hell is wrong with the kid. Is this something to do with aliens…U.F.O.'s…what?"

Franklin smirked slightly. "I *can* talk about the boy's condition," he said. "Though I don't know how much I can add to what you probably already know. There is a foreign substance in his bloodstream—something I've never seen before. It's spreading throughout his body and his cells and genetic makeup seem to be…changing."

"Changing?" Cochran asked, glancing past the doctor and to Kurt. "Does this have something to do with the meteor?"

Doctor Franklin's eyes widened. "The meteor! Yes, tell me about the meteor," he said. "Dr. White said that there was a substance reported to be seeping from it?"

"Yeah," Cochran replied. "Kurt's friend was there…witnessed the whole thing. He says something leaked from a large crack in the meteor. Some sort of glowing goo. It got onto Kurt and his friend seems to believe that it may have done something to him."

"Interesting," Franklin said, stroking his chin. "Did you believe him?"

Cochran looked at him, obviously taken aback. "About the glowing goo? Hell no," he quipped. "The boys were out there drinking. I saw no traces of anything like that when I examined the meteor for myself."

Suddenly, Marie reappeared, now adorning a mask, surgical cap, gloves, and disposable scrubs.

"Go over to him," Doctor Franklin said. "But please don't touch him. See if he will respond to your voice."

Marie nodded and quickly moved to Kurt's bedside. His eyes were open, but he was staring at the ceiling…seemingly at nothing. She leaned in close and said, "Hey Kurt, it's Marie. I'm here now. Can you hear me?"

Sheriff Cochran looked on and noticed Kurt blink once. The boy's eyes shifted slightly, as if he were trying to look over at his sister. It seemed that he was unable to move his head. Marie noticed it too and moved so that he could see her better.

"What happened to you, Kurt?" she asked. "Can you talk?"

Kurt stared at his sister, his eyes widening slightly. The monitor beside him displayed an increase in his heart rate.

"He can't talk," she said, looking back at Doctor Franklin. "He hears me, and he understands me...I can see it in his eyes. He just can't talk to me."

Dr. Franklin didn't reply. He just stared at Kurt, his face revealing nothing. Marie returned her attention to her brother.

"Did something happen to you in the woods?" she asked.

Kurt's eyes darted around wildly, and his heart rate increased even more. Marie considered what to say or do next when suddenly something strange caught her eye. "When is the last time you shaved?" she asked, smiling at Kurt.

Her brother's eyes revealed nothing this time, it was as if he'd never even heard a question.

"Have you noticed this?" Marie asked, looking back at Doctor Franklin. "These fine hairs on his face...even on his forehead. What the hell is this?"

Doctor Franklin strolled over and stood next to her. He turned on an overhead light and peered closely at Kurt's face. Sure enough, his face was covered in fine hairs...dark in color.

"That wasn't there when he arrived," he muttered. "Interesting..."

"What the hell would cause that?" Marie asked aggressively. "You're doing tests on him. What is wrong with him?"

Doctor Franklin sighed and gently placed a hand on Marie's shoulder. "We're trying to figure that out," he said. "Your brother is undergoing some sort of biological change. We're running tests trying to figure out what exactly it is, but clearly something is amiss. Why don't you go home and rest up for a few hours? Come back later today and maybe we'll know more. There is nothing you can do for him right now."

"And then something could happen while I'm away," Marie said, looking back over at Kurt. "No thanks, I'll stay right here."

Doctor Franklin looked over at Sheriff Cochran, clearly wanting him to help out.

"Uh, Marie," Cochran said, taking a step forward. "I think the doc is right. You told me yourself you've been up all night wondering where Kurt was. If you're gonna be there for him, you need to get some rest. How 'bout I take you home, so you can wash up, take a good nap, and then I'll bring you back this afternoon?"

Marie looked over at him and now more than ever he could see the exhaustion in her eyes. She took a deep breath and at that moment seemed defeated. "I suppose you're right," she muttered. She then glanced back at Doctor Franklin. "If I go, then you swear to call me if something happens."

"Of course," Franklin replied. "You've got my word on that."

Marie looked to Cochran. It was as if she was wanting him to tell her if she could believe him or not.

"Honey, he'll call you," he said. "And he's gonna call me too because I want to stay in the loop with what's going on here."

She considered it a moment more before finally leaning in close to her brother again. "Kurt, I'm gonna go home for a bit but I swear I'll be back this afternoon. You hang in there, bud."

Then she stood and made her way back to the door, snatching the cap and mask away from her face. "Get me out of here before I change my mind," she said to Cochran as she strode past.

The sheriff looked over at Doctor Franklin once more. "We *will* be back," he said firmly. "And I'm gonna expect more answers than what you're giving me right now."

The doctor bit his lip and nodded as they disappeared into the hallway. When he was certain they were gone he glanced at the nurse nearest him. "Get the restraints and make sure he is secured to this bed," he muttered. She nodded and went about the task. Franklin then stared at Kurt a long moment before finally reaching over and placing a hand on the side of the boy's face. He used his thumb to pull up the upper lip to get a look at his teeth. He took a deep breath and stared in disbelief. The teeth he was looking at no longer appeared human. They were becoming sharper...pointier, and it was getting worse.

CHAPTER 6

Much to her surprise, Marie had no trouble falling asleep. She was the epitome of exhausted and despite her mind racing a million miles a minute, no sooner had her head hit the pillow, did she drift off to sleep. She probably would have slept longer had it not been for the sudden knocking—or pounding, rather—on the front door. With a mixture of frustration and grogginess, Marie swung her legs off the bed and willed them to carry her to the door.

She grabbed the knob, then thought better of it and peeked out of the living room window to see who was there. The pounding continued, and she guessed it was either someone really angry with her, or someone that was really scared. Slowly, she pulled the curtain back and breathed a sigh of relief when she saw it was Tony Joyner.

Marie snatched the door open and as expected, found Tony standing on the doormat. He was wide-eyed, and his face was ashen.

"Tony Joyner you better have a good reason for beating on my door like you're the police or—"

"We've got to go get Kurt," he interrupted. His eyes darted over at the neighbor's house and then back to Marie. "He shouldn't be at that lab."

Marie squinted and cocked her head. "Wait, slow down," she said calmly. "Where is all of this coming from? The lab is trying to help him."

Tony closed his eyes and clearly was struggling to keep calm. "No," he said firmly. "They want you to think that but they're running tests on him—and not the kind of tests that are going to help him. They want to study him...I'm telling you we gotta get him out of there."

Marie looked down the street in both directions. There was something about the way Tony kept looking around them that troubled her. She grabbed his shoulder.

"Get in here," she said, pulling him forward.

With the door shut, Marie leaned her back against it and narrowed her eyes at Tony. She pointed at the nearby sofa and he sat.

"Talk," she snapped.

Tony rubbed his knees a minute as if he were trying again to calm himself. Finally, he took a deep breath and began. "Okay, so do you know that kid Kyle Simpson?"

Marie's brow furrowed, and she pursed her lips as she thought. After a moment she said, "Umm...should I?"

Tony rolled his eyes in frustration and shifted on the sofa. "Yes, he's in my class...and Kurt's. I wouldn't call him a friend, but his mom is the librarian at the school."

"Oh yes," she said, remembering. "Mrs. Simpson was always a bitch to me—I've tried to block her out of my memory."

"What?" Tony said, clearly confused.

Marie shook her head. "It doesn't matter," she replied. "Go on."

"Well, Kyle's dad works at Walker Laboratory—where they took Kurt."

Marie bit her lip and felt her heart skip a beat. "Go on," she said, not sure she really wanted to know where this conversation was going.

Tony stood up from the sofa and began pacing. Marie watched him for almost a full minute before he continued. "Kyle called me this afternoon. He said he heard his mom and dad talking earlier this morning…they didn't know he was listening in the other room. He told me that his dad mentioned Kurt by name and said that there was a terrible situation going on at the lab and that if Kurt survived he'd never be allowed to leave the lab."

Marie crossed her arms and felt a bit faint. She tried to tell herself that the information she was hearing was second-hand and though Tony was a very trustworthy kid, she knew nothing about Kyle Simpson. "What else did he say?" she asked.

Tony chewed his lip as he pondered her question a moment. "Well, he told me not to say anything and he was just trying to find out what was going on since he knew me and Kurt were buds. He said whatever happened to him was a pretty big deal and that he'd never heard his dad so upset before."

"Did you tell him about the meteor?" Marie asked.

Tony shook his head. "No, and honestly, I only didn't because I was so freaked out about what he told me." He paused and squinted at her. "I take it you're glad I didn't mention it?"

She nodded. "Right...don't say anything about what you saw to anyone. I think right now the less people that know, the better."

Tony looked at her, clearly puzzled. "I don't get it," he said. "I figured the more people that know he's over there, the better. The lab can't keep it hidden from everyone in town."

"Yes, but I don't need what we're planning to get out and get back to someone at the lab."

Tony swallowed, his Adam's apple bobbing. "And what are we planning?" he asked reluctantly.

She took a deep breath and ran slender fingers through her brown hair. "You said it yourself," she replied. "We've got to go get him."

Tony remained on the couch while Marie retreated to her bedroom. She made a beeline for her closet and reached around on the top shelf until she found what she was looking for. When she pulled her hand out, there was a black handgun clutched in it. She ejected the magazine to make sure it was loaded and then slammed it back into the grip. After placing the gun in the back of her waistband she made her way to the nightstand beside her bed and retrieved a flashlight.

When she returned to the living room, Tony was standing near the front door.

"Does your mom know you're here?" Marie asked him.

He put his hands in his pockets and shifted his feet.

"I take that to mean she doesn't," Marie said, looking away from him and snatching her car keys off a hook in the wall.

"My mom is asleep," Tony said. "She works nights and she's kinda used to me doing my own thing during the day."

"Well you still should tell her what you're up to," Marie said, reaching for the door. "You need to go home and stay out of this. I appreciate the information you gave me."

Marie exited the house and made her way along the sidewalk that led to the blue muscle car parked in the driveway, Tony in tow.

"No," he called after her. "I'm going with you. You're gonna need help and he may be your brother but he's my best friend."

"Go home, Tony," Marie said as she climbed into the car.

Tony snatched open the passenger door and plopped down on the seat beside her. "No, the only place I'm going is with you," he snapped. "I know him better than you and I was there when that stuff in the meteor got on him."

Marie rolled her eyes and clenched her teeth. "Tony, sweetie, don't be a nut rash. Get the hell out of my car and go home. I'm not going to be held responsible if something happens to you."

Tony glared at her but didn't budge. He instead reached over his shoulder and fastened his seatbelt. "We're wasting time," he said.

Marie sighed deeply and gripped the steering wheel hard in frustration. After considering her options for a moment, she finally turned the key and the Chevelle roared to life. "Fine," she growled, pulling the stick into reverse. "But if you get your ass killed, don't blame me."

She mashed the accelerator and the car lurched backward just as Sheriff Ray Cochran's patrol car rolled to a stop at the end of the drive.

"Dammit," Marie grumbled, putting the car back into park. She watched in the rearview mirror as Cochran exited his vehicle and strolled up to the driver's side window of her car. He glanced in at her and she watched as his eyes drifted past her and over to Tony. Marie rolled the window down.

"Hi sheriff," she said, smiling.

He smiled back. "Marie, I thought we were going back to the lab together."

She nodded. "Oh yeah," she said. "Honestly, I forgot all about that. I figured you were busy anyway...I'm sure you've got more to do than worry about my brother."

"Oh, it's no trouble," Cochran replied. "Tony, how are you doing?"

Tony smiled nervously. "Doing good, Sheriff," he said.

"You going to the lab with Marie?"

Tony nodded. "Yeah, just concerned about Kurt."

Sheriff Cochran rubbed at the graying stubble on his chin and moved his eyes back and forth between Marie and Tony. "Alright," he said finally. "Let's head on over. You guys follow me in case the fella at the guard shack gives us any trouble."

Marie smiled. "Sounds good," she said.

Cochran nodded and then returned to his car. Marie rolled the window up quickly, cursing under her breath.

"Why didn't you just tell him what I told you?" Tony asked.

Marie put the car in reverse and backed into the street. "Oh, I don't know Tony," she quipped. "Because it sounds batshit crazy?"

The sun was drifting lazily toward the western sky as Marie's blue Chevelle rumbled loudly in the wake of Cochran's boxy patrol car. There were orange and yellow leaves littering the road on the country road that led to the laboratory and they swirled and danced behind the cars as they navigated the curves and hills of Baker County.

"You know, I've never even seen this place before," Tony said as Marie turned the car next to a sign that said WALKER LABORATORY AHEAD—AUTHORIZED PERSONNEL ONLY.

"You're not missing anything," she answered. "It's just an old gray building in the middle of nowhere—it looks outdated."

"Do you think the rumors about the place are true?" he asked.

She looked at him with a sideways glance. "Which rumors? The ones about the aliens or the U.F.O.'s?"

He smiled at her. "Both."

She stared out the windshield as she considered the question. There was a time that she'd have laughed at such a suggestion. Now, however, she wasn't so sure.

"I don't know what to think right now," she answered. "All I know right now is that I want my brother back and I'm going to do whatever I have to do to make that happen."

Tony stared at her a moment but couldn't think of anything helpful to say. He instead turned his attention ahead to Sheriff Cochran's patrol car as it approached a large sinister looking gray building surrounded by pine trees. Once he stopped at the guard shack, he leaned out of the window and chatted a moment with a man that appeared to be in his thirties.

"That's not the same guard we spoke to last night," Marie said softly.

Sheriff Cochran and the guard spoke for much longer than she expected. At one point, the sheriff leaned further out of the window and looked back toward Marie, pointing at her. The guard looked at her and then back to Cochran. Finally, the guard opened the gate, but he didn't seem happy about it. Marie nodded at him as she followed the sheriff through. The guard stared at her with an icy gaze that seemed to pierce right through her.

Once the two cars were parked in the same area of the lot where Cochran had parked the night before, Marie quickly got out of her car and retrieved a denim jacket from the back seat. She put it on and made sure to pull the back of it down low to ensure that the gun she was carrying was concealed.

"Do you think they have metal detectors in there?" Tony whispered, noticing what she was doing.

"Keep quiet," Marie snapped at him, though she had to admit he asked a good question.

She thought back to the night before when she and the sheriff had ventured inside the building. It was all such a blur and she could not remember walking through a metal detector.

"What was that all about?" Marie asked Cochran as they drew near him.

The sheriff shook his head and his brow furrowed with disgust. "I swear, you'd think they're hiding Frankenstein's monster in there or something," he complained. "It took an act of Congress just to get that fool to call his supervisor to confirm what I was telling him. He didn't want to let us in."

The revelation was not a comforting one for Marie, but she held her tongue on the matter. Instead, she decided to go ahead and make her intentions known to Cochran—or at least some of them.

"I want to take Kurt home," she said as they briskly made their way up the sidewalk that led to the sliding glass door entrance. "And don't try to talk me out of it, my mind is made up."

They were walking side by side with Tony behind them. Sheriff Cochran glanced over at Marie. "Even if it's not what's best for him?" he asked.

She closed her eyes a moment and licked her lips. "Sheriff, do you *really* think they've got Kurt's best interests in mind right now? That Dr. Franklin seemed shady as hell."

Cochran smirked. "Yeah, I can't argue with that, Marie," he said. "But I saw no evidence that they were doing anything to hurt your brother. And why would they? They know I'm involved and could cause all sorts of trouble for them if I found out something was amiss."

"I know that's what you believe," Marie replied. "But sheriff, this place is funded by the federal government and no one really knows what's going on in here."

Sheriff Cochran wanted to discuss the matter further, but they'd reached the entrance and quickly stepped inside. There was a different guard to greet them inside too, though he appeared much friendlier than the man at the guard shack.

"Welcome sheriff," he said, shaking the larger man's hand.

The guard then politely shook Marie and Tony's hands as well. He was blonde with blue eyes, tall and slender.

"Dr. Franklin said to expect you," he said. "I guess I should've shared that with Frank," he then added, his gaze moving beyond them and to the guard shack down the hill. "I apologize for the confusion."

"How's the boy?" Cochran asked, getting down to business.

"I'm afraid I'm not privy to that information," the guard replied.

Marie heard them talking, but her thoughts were elsewhere. She noticed the metal detector just behind where the guard was standing. It was the large walk-through kind and as she stared at it intensely she felt a bead of sweat roll down her back.

"Follow me and I'll take you to him," the guard said, and he turned and walked toward the metal detector. He then paused and looked at the sheriff. "Y'all just step around it—I know what you're carrying," he said with a chuckle.

Marie breathed a sigh of relief as she and Tony followed Cochran around the metal detector. Tony looked at her, his forehead beaded with perspiration. It had apparently been a stressful moment for him as well.

"Dr Franklin's office is at the end of the hall, on the left," the guard said, pointing down the corridor.

Sheriff Cochran extended his thanks and then led Marie and Tony down the hallway.

"This is where he was," Marie said, pausing next to a closed door on the right side.

Cochran looked at it curiously and soon realized that it was indeed the room where Kurt had been the night before. He looked at Marie and could see the concern on her face. Without saying a word, he reached for the knob and opened the door. The two of them peered into the room and found only an empty bed, neatly made up with clean linens.

"What the hell?" he muttered softly.

Marie looked over at him and he could see her green eyes darkening.

"I'm sure there's a good explanation," he said, trying to reassure her. "I'll get to the bottom of it."

Marie bit her lip and Tony patted her on the back.

"They probably just moved him to another room," he said, trying to do his part to keep her calm.

Another thirty feet or so led them to an open door on the left side of the hallway. Cochran stepped through and sat down on the cushy leather chair directly in front of the large wooden desk where Dr. Franklin was seated.

The doctor rose from where he was sitting and immediately offered a handshake to Marie. She reluctantly took it and then sat down beside Cochran. With no other seats available, Tony leaned against the door jamb and crossed his arms.

"Now I'm sure you're wondering where he is," Franklin said quickly.

"It crossed my mind, yeah," Marie snapped at him. "Where is my brother, doctor?"

"Well," he said as he returned to his chair. "There's been a...development."

Marie arched an eyebrow. "What sort of development?" she asked, trying desperately to keep her composure.

Doctor Franklin took a deep breath and steepled his fingers in front of his face. "Well, let's just say that your brother is undergoing some neurological changes that require more testing downstairs," he said nonchalantly. "When he's finished, we'll bring him back to his room."

"Okay," Marie replied coolly. "How long will the testing take?"

Franklin's gaze drifted away from her and down to his wristwatch. "Sure...umm, I'd say another six hours or so. He just went back."

"Six hours?" Cochran asked gruffly. "What the hell is going on with him? What sort of neurological changes are you talking about?"

Doctor Franklin shifted uneasily in his chair, but his face remained stoic. "He's undergoing some changes unlike anything I've ever seen before. Just let us run these tests and I promise you that you can see him."

"I want to see him right now," Marie said, glaring at him.

Doctor Franklin held up his hands apologetically. "I know that, Marie," he said softly. "And I want you to see him, but please understand he needs our help and—"

"Right now," Marie said abruptly.

Sheriff Cochran looked over at her curiously, then slowly returned his gaze to Doctor Franklin. "You heard her," he said. "She's his sister and she wants to see him."

Franklin smiled and took a deep breath through his nose. "I'm afraid that's not going to be possible," he said. "I just can't—"

"Can't? Or won't?" Marie asked, narrowing her eyes sharply.

The doctor's warm expression suddenly changed to something much colder. "You won't like what you see," he said flatly. "Come back tomorrow and I'll let you see him…that's a promise."

Marie crossed her arms and shifted her weight in the chair. She looked over at Sheriff Cochran, her mouth a straight line. Cochran read what she was thinking and leaned forward onto the desk.

"Doc, we want to see the kid right now," he said.

Doctor Franklin shook his head. "I'm afraid I can't let you do that—and there is no legal obligation for me to let you see him either."

Cochran was taken aback and made no attempt to hide it. "Are you kidding me?" he snarled. "I'm the damn law around here and I want to see him. This is his next of kin."

Franklin looked over at Marie. "Are you Kurt's legal guardian?"

"You're damn right I am," she snapped back.

"Can you prove it?" the doctor asked.

Marie's mouth dropped opened slightly and she again looked to Sheriff Cochran.

"Let me see the boy," the sheriff said, rising from his chair.

"Sheriff, you need to calm down and you need to sit down, right now," Franklin said, looking up at him.

"The only thing I'm doing right now," Cochran growled, "is going to see Kurt Bledsoe. Now take me to him or I'll find him myself."

Doctor Franklin pinched the bridge of his nose and rubbed his eyes. "I don't have time for this," he whispered, and he then reached for the phone on his desk. "Yes, I need security in my office right now," he said.

Sheriff Cochran looked down at Marie and grabbed her arm, helping her up. "Come on," he said. "Let's go find Kurt."

"Sheriff, I'm warning you to stop right there," Franklin said, he himself now rising from his desk. "The security guards in this building are armed and will use whatever means necessary to keep what we do here protected."

Sheriff Cochran paused and glared at him. "And just what is it that you do here, doc?" he asked, turning his head slightly. "What the hell are you hiding in the basement?"

"Sheriff, we need to go," Tony said suddenly. He was looking down the hallway.

Marie and Cochran stepped out just in time to see four armed guards charging toward them. One of them was the blonde man they'd met in the lobby.

"Stop right there!" he called out.

Sheriff Cochran glanced over at both Tony and Marie. "Follow me," he said. "Stay close!"

They disappeared around the corner at the end of the hall and the guards stopped momentarily at Doctor Franklin's doorway.

"What's going on?" the blonde guard asked.

"They're asking too many questions," Franklin replied with disgust. "They're demanding to see the subject. They've taken it too far now and cannot leave this building."

The blonde guard looked at him quizzically. "But sir, he's the sheriff of the county."

The doctor's eyebrows raised slightly. "And law enforcement is a dangerous job," he said. "The situation couldn't be more perfect. The sister, the sheriff, and the only real witness of what happened last night are all in the building. We keep them contained here and our secrets stay here. Do not let them leave and use whatever means necessary to do so."

The guard blinked and nodded. "We'll make sure, sir," he said.

"In the meantime," Franklin continued, "the building is going on lockdown."

The doctor grabbed a key from his desk drawer and unlocked a panel on the wall next to a wooden bookshelf. Behind the panel there were a series of switches, similar to what one would find in a breaker box. Franklin began flipping the switches and a rumble began to echo throughout the building. In mere seconds, every window and every door to the outside world became closed off by a retractable steel shutter that slid down from an overhead slot.

CHAPTER 7

The fluorescent lighting flickered overhead and there was a rumble that seemed to be coming from all directions. It was so loud and ominous that the ground underneath their feet vibrated.

"What the hell was that?" Marie asked as she chased after Sheriff Cochran.

"I don't know," Cochran answered as he pulled his sidearm from its holster. "We'll worry about that later...right now we need to find your brother."

They were running down another corridor that was much like the one they'd just left. Every several feet there was a wooden door...all of them closed. This time however, there was an elevator at the midway point that caught Cochran's eye. He paused and slapped the button indicating that they wanted to go down.

"Are you sure he's down there?" Marie asked, glancing over her shoulder to see if they were being chased again.

"The doc mentioned that he was downstairs," Cochran answered, and he slapped the button again. "It's not much but it's all we have to go on right now. Come on dammit," he grumbled at the steel doors.

"Uh guys, we've got company," Tony stammered.

Cochran looked to his left and the four guards that were chasing them had just rounded the corner.

"Stop right there, Sheriff!" the blonde guard shouted.

Cochran noticed he was holding a gun and he felt his hand tighten around the grip of his own. "Come on," he told Marie and Tony. "We gotta keep moving."

"They've got guns," Tony said as he chased after the sheriff.

"Yeah, and so do I...now keep up," Cochran barked.

The trio kept running and the echoing footsteps of their pursuers rang loudly in their ears. At the end of the hallway they suddenly had a choice to make...right or left.

"Look!" Marie shouted suddenly, and she pointed at a sign on the wall to their left that indicated a nearby stairwell.

Cochran said nothing but began running again. They'd only gone twenty feet when he found a metal door that was positioned back toward the interior of the building. It had a window and he could clearly see the stairwell beyond it. "This way," he said, pushing the door open forcefully with his shoulder.

They began racing down the steps and to their surprise the stairwell seemed to go down several levels—much farther than any of them would've guessed.

"My god, where do we stop?" Marie asked with despair.

Suddenly a gunshot rang out from above them. The sound was loud and thunderous to the point their ears were ringing. Cochran pushed Marie and Tony behind him and pointed his weapon upward.

"Hold your fire!" he shouted. "I'm a law enforcement officer and I'm telling you right now to put that gun away!"

"No one has to get hurt, Sheriff," the blonde guard shouted down at him. "We just need you to surrender right now. Put that gun down and let's talk about this."

"There is no scenario where I'm putting my gun down," Cochran snapped back. "I'm the sheriff here—I'm the one with the authority here."

There was a chuckle and though Cochran couldn't see him, he could tell it was the blonde guard. "Sheriff I don't know how to tell you this, but this building is out of your jurisdiction. You have no power here. This is a federal facility and that badge on your chest don't mean a damn thing."

Cochran bit his lip and snorted in disgust. He looked over his shoulder at the door closest to him. They'd only gone down three levels, but it seemed their chances were going to be a lot better if they got out of the stairwell.

"Listen to me," he whispered to Marie and Tony. "I want you to open that door but do it as quietly as you can. Open it and go through it. I'll be right behind you."

Marie nodded and reached for the handle. She paused a moment and read the signage just below the window. It read: CONTAINMENT, LEVEL 3. She and Tony looked at each other and after a quick glance into the window they proceeded to open the door.

Sheriff Cochran meanwhile kept his attention on the stairs above him.

"Listen," he said. "You're trying to reason with me so I'm gonna try to reason with you now. I've got no intention of allowing myself, or my companions to be taken into your custody. Now, you can allow us to leave or I'm going to make you let us leave…it's your choice."

There was more laughter from above, this time more maniacal. Cochran glanced over his shoulder to see that Tony was holding the door open for him. Slowly, the sheriff backed through the door and then lightly allowed the door to close. There was an empty desk across from the door they'd just passed through, and behind it an old wooden chair. Cochran quickly grabbed the chair and then wedged it tightly under the door handle to prevent—or at least hinder—the guards from continuing their pursuit.

"Alright, let's keep moving," he said.

It was at that moment he noticed Marie was holding a gun.

"Where the hell did you get that?" he asked, pointing at the weapon.

She smiled sheepishly. "I told you I was coming to get my brother out of here and I was going to do it no matter what," she said.

Sheriff Cochran looked up from the gun and met Marie's eyes. Part of him wanted to scold her. Most of him wanted to thank her. "Come on," he said, finally opting on saying nothing more on the matter.

They found themselves in yet another hallway, but this one was flanked with glass windows, and beyond the windows there were people in white lab coats working.

"Just be calm," Cochran said as they casually walked by.

Out of the corner of her eye, Marie could see some of the people looking at them…watching them. "They see us," she whispered.

"Makes no difference to me," Cochran said. "Don't be flashing that gun around and we have nothing to worry—"

"Excuse me," a man of Asian descent said suddenly. He'd stepped out of a doorway ahead of where they were going. "May I help you?"

The man was Marie's height and his black hair was combed neatly with a well-defined part. He was wearing safety glasses and latex gloves.

"Yeah, uh, I'm looking for someone," Cochran stammered. "A young kid…Kurt Bledsoe. Doctor Franklin told me we could find him down here?"

The man eyed him suspiciously. "Franklin said you could find him on level three?"

"He just told us we could find him downstairs," Marie said suddenly. "He got tied up on a phone call, so we decided to head on down—we had no idea there were multiple levels."

The man opened his mouth slightly and nodded as if the explanation was beginning to make sense. "I see," he said. "Well I know you mean well but I assure you that Doctor Franklin would not approve of you venturing down here without an escort." He paused and looked them over more closely. "And where are your visitor badges?"

Cochran pulled back his jacket revealing the gold star on his chest. "I guess Franklin figured this one would suffice," he said with a wry smile.

The man smiled at him but there was a nervousness—an uneasiness, that wasn't there moments before. "Sheriff, I think you should return to the first floor. This level is not safe."

Cochran looked around him and chuckled. "Really? Why not? You hiding a monster around here or something?"

The man didn't smile back. Before he could say anything else there was a loud banging emanating from the door that Cochran had wedged shut with the chair.

"Okay, I think Kurt Bledsoe, the young man you're looking for is being held on level four. You don't have access to that level without an escort. I'm going to have to ask you to please return to the first floor and await Doctor Franklin's assistance."

The banging on the door continued, this time louder. The man looked past Sheriff Cochran toward the end of the hallway. The door could not be seen from where they were standing but clearly, he knew where the sound was coming from.

"Please wait right here," he said, moving around them.

Sheriff Cochran waited until the man disappeared around the corner and then he again urged Marie and Tony to follow him. They were running again and didn't stop until they reached the end of the hallway. There was a red door embedded in the wall, but otherwise it was a dead end.

"What now?" Marie asked, looking around them. "We're trapped."

"We go the only place we can go," Cochran answered. "Through this door."

"Wait," Tony said, sounding somewhat panicked. "There's something really creepy about this place and I've got a bad feeling about this door."

Cochran grabbed the boy by the arm and jerked him close. "Yeah? Well I've got a bad feeling about the armed guards that are gonna appear on the other end of this hall any second. What's your problem with this door?"

Tony swallowed, and his eyes moved away from the sheriff and to the door. "It's not like the other doors," he said. "It's metal, not wood. And it's red..."

Cochran looked to Marie who shrugged in response, then back to Tony. "So what?" he asked, dumbfounded.

"Well, I—I just think that since this particular door is metal and painted red, then it could potentially mean there is something dangerous behind it," he said.

At that moment a thunderous boom echoed loudly from the other end of the hall followed by a spark and loud clang off the metal door, mere feet away from where the sheriff was standing. Cochran looked at the door and noticed a slight indentation where a bullet had struck, but failed to penetrate, it.

"That was a warning shot," the blonde guard called out. "Put down your weapon!"

Without further hesitation, Cochran twisted the knob and pushed the door. He half expected it to be locked but was pleasantly surprised to find that it wasn't. He nearly fell as he entered the room. Marie and Tony ran into his back as he stopped suddenly.

"Shut the door!" Cochran commanded.

"Are you sure?" Tony asked.

Marie kicked the door closed with her foot and immediately the three of them became enveloped in pitch black darkness. There was a *click* sound that originated from the door and Marie, knowing exactly what it meant, reached for the knob to get confirmation.

"It's locked," she said. "We're locked in here."

"I knew it," Tony said. "I knew it, I knew it…"

"Shut up," Cochran growled. "I can't see a damn thing…can either of you see anything?"

Before anyone could answer, floodlights on the ceiling came on, washing them all suddenly in warm light. It became so bright, the three of them had to squint and give their eyes a moment to adjust.

"Sheriff Cochran," a familiar voice called out from somewhere above. It was Doctor Franklin and his voice seemed to be emanating from a speaker.

"Yeah?" Cochran asked, looking up in all directions.

"I tried very hard to make sure we would not find ourselves on the path we're now on," Franklin said. "But here we are."

Marie's eyes had finally adjusted to the bright light and she quickly surveyed her surroundings. The room where they now found themselves was rectangular and the back wall was lined with eight metal doors, each with a small rectangular slot near the floor, and another slot near the top of the door, roughly the size of a loaf of bread. The slot at the top of each door was fitted with bars spaced roughly six inches apart all the way across. Through one of the slots, she saw movement.

"And what path is that?" Cochran asked. His eyes drifted away from the ceiling and to the eight cells that Marie had noticed.

"What's in there?" Tony asked in a voice just above a whisper.

"You wanted to know what we're hiding in the basement," Franklin answered. "Well—you're about to find out!"

CHAPTER 8

"We need to find a way out of here," Cochran said, a hint of panic in his voice.

"There's a hatch over there," Tony said, pointing to a yellow protrusion, rectangular in shape, coming out of the floor.

Cochran said nothing, but instead ran toward the hatch Tony had pointed out. He didn't wait to see if Marie and Tony had followed. In his mind he knew that if there was a chance any of them was going to survive, every second had to count. He dropped to his knees and immediately reached for a small handle on the side of it. He pulled, and his heart sank as he came to the realization that it was locked.

At that moment there were several loud *clacks* that rang out in unison. The three of them paused, dead in their tracks, and turned toward the eight cells to their right. All the doors swung open at the same time and for a long moment all any of them could see was the black interior of the cells and nothing more.

Upon closer inspection, Cochran found a padlock on the side of the hatch. "Step back," he barked as he pointed his gun at the lock.

There was a thunderous *BOOM* followed by the subtle clinking of the broken lock falling to the cement floor.

"Oh my god…oh my god," Marie whispered. "What the hell are those?"

Cochran whipped his head around and redirected his attention to the open cells again. What he saw made his jaw drop. Tony had moved behind him and placed his back against the wall. The color had completely drained from his face and he looked as though he was on the verge of fainting.

"Wood apes," Cochran said finally, disbelief evident in his voice. "They say those things have been in Baker County for a long time."

"T—The gunshot didn't even scare them," Tony stammered.

The creatures were all similar in appearance, but their hair color and facial features varied. A couple of them were almost black, while most were different shades of brown. There was even one that was gray in color and appeared to be the oldest of all. While they all had ape-like features, a couple of the smaller ones took on a softer, more feminine appearance. It was Cochran's estimation that they were indeed female but no less menacing than their male counterparts.

All the wood apes glared at the three humans with a look of pure hatred. Their black eyes were locked on them and displayed a mixture of rage and curiosity. It was the curiosity that Cochran picked up on and knew would give them the window of opportunity for escape. Without hesitation, he flung the heavy metal hatch open and it clanged loudly on the concrete.

"Let's go, now," he snapped, motioning for Marie to come toward him.

She did and quickly shuffled down a ladder into the blackness below. Tony followed and was shaking so badly Cochran could feel the ladder vibrating with his every move. As soon as there was room, Sheriff Cochran clambered down after them and then whirled around quickly to make sure they weren't being pursued. The wood apes were standing around the hatch opening, forming a semi-circle. They had definitely closed in but did not seem to be in any great hurry. Cochran pulled the hatch down over his head as he descended the rungs of the ladder. He spun the large wheel on the bottom side of the door and when he was satisfied it was latched, he continued down to where he eventually caught up to Marie and Tony.

"They're gonna come after us," Marie said, her voice sounding panicked.

"No, they're not," Cochran replied firmly. "The hatch is locked."

"And what's to keep them from unlocking it the same way you did?" she rebutted.

Cochran scratched at the side of his neck, he was sweating profusely. So much in fact, he decided to shed his coat, tossing it aside. "That's a good point," he admitted, glancing back up the ladder from where they'd just come.

"Then we need to keep moving," Tony said, sounding even more panicked than Marie.

"And we will," Cochran replied. "I'm sure that Franklin has got his goons rounding up those things right now."

***

"Get them back into their cells!" Franklin barked loudly over the two-way radio.

The blonde security guard, a man named Michael Lynch, rolled his eyes and cursed under his breath. He then opened the mic and replied, "Why the hell did you let those things out, doc?"

There was static, and then, "Not for you to question," Franklin barked back. "Get them into their cells before they try something. This isn't something you haven't done before!"

Franklin was right. Lynch and his men had a lot of experience wrangling the wood apes and getting them to follow orders. The high-voltage cattle prods helped their efforts and the creatures had gained a healthy respect for the tool when they saw it. On the other hand, he could think of no time where he'd had to wrangle eight of them at once.

"You heard him," Lynch spat angrily as he turned to face the other two guards that flanked him. "Let's get this done quick and in a hurry."

Lynch reached for a large keychain that dangled from his belt loop. He thumbed through the ring until he found the key he was looking for and then made his way over to a panel on the wall beside the door. He inserted a key and the panel swung open to reveal the cattle prods they would need to take care of the matter.

Each guard grabbed one and then Lynch retrieved yet another key to open the door. He inserted it and then paused to glance over his shoulder at the other men.

"Don't forget what these damn things are," he said. "Don't turn your back on them and light them up the second one of them gets out of line. Are we clear?"

The men nodded and when he was ready, Lynch turned the key and opened the door. Once in the room, they quickly shut the door behind them and made sure it locked. The wood apes were gathered around the hatch in the floor and one of them was trying to turn the wheel on top of it to open the door.

"Okay, let's get back in the cells!" Lynch yelled, and as he did so all the wood apes turned to look at him in unison.

The one that had been trying to open the hatch, stood up and Lynch estimated he was nearly eight feet tall. His hair was dark— almost black, and his eyes were so black they were hard to find in the hair.

Lynch glanced at his two counterparts and gestured for them to close in with his chin. The three men carefully moved forward and as they did, the wood apes began to chatter amongst themselves. They all sounded panicked, or worried, all except the big dark one.

"Get back in your cells now," Lynch demanded, and he pointed toward the open cells with the cattle prod.

Two of the wood apes noticed the cattle prod and immediately moved away from the rest of the group toward their respective cells.

"The others aren't moving," one of the guards said.

"I can see that," Lynch grumbled. "Light 'em up."

The two guards nodded and briskly moved toward the wood apes closest to them. Without hesitation they thrust the prods forward and as soon as they made contact, both wood apes howled in pain and scrambled away frantically toward the cells. Lynch roared with laughter and then popped another one with his own prod, getting the same result.

The remaining three wood apes glared at him with an intensity that he could literally feel wash over him. "Get those cells closed," Lynch said.

One of the guards moved toward the cells but no sooner had he taken two steps, one of the wood apes darted toward him and then stood in his path.

Lynch smiled and shook his head. "Light his ass up," he said, chuckling.

The guard made a motion to do just that, but the wood ape reacted with a lightning fast movement, ripping the prod from his grasp and hurtling it through the air where it struck the far wall of the room. The cattle prod broke into two pieces and clanged loudly when it struck the cement floor.

"Dammit," Lynch said, as he reached for his sidearm.

The other ape that had been standing alongside the dark one over the hatch, moved just as fast and swung its large hairy arm forward making direct contact with Lynch's back. He was hurtled forward and crashed hard into the chest of the dark wood ape that had been trying to open the hatch. Without hesitation he raised his gun and pulled the trigger. The blast thundered loudly but missed because the dark wood ape had caught him by the wrist and pushed the weapon aside just as he fired.

Suddenly, Lynch heard screaming behind him and turned his head just in time to see the guard that had lost his cattle prod jerked forward by his collar. The wood ape he'd attacked had grabbed him and when he pulled him close, the creature proceeded to grab both of the guard's arms at the same time, ripping them from the man's torso.

Lynch could hear a ripping, tearing sound when the gruesome act unfolded, and he closed his eyes, unable to look. At that moment, another gunshot rang out from behind him. It was the other guard, Lynch knew, and he heard the man scream. The scream was loud, blood curdling, and then it was cut off immediately as if someone had turned off a stereo in the middle of a song. There was another horrific sound—a crunching sound and in his mind's eye Lynch could see the guard's throat being crushed by a hairy hand.

With his eyes still closed, Lynch felt himself being pulled from the ground by the front of his shirt. Terrified, but unwilling to quit, he thrust his cattle prod forward and into the chest of the large dark wood ape that had him. There was a hum of electricity, the smell of burnt hair, and a howl of pain—or possibly rage.

Lynch was immediately released, and he fortunately landed on his feet. He then ran with all his might toward the red metal door that would grant him safety. It was locked, he knew, and when he was mere feet away, he reached for the key ring on his belt only to find that it was gone. As he slammed into the door, he grabbed at the knob and frantically tried to get out, though he knew the effort was futile.

"Open the damn door!" Lynch screamed, knowing full well that Franklin could hear his pleas.

"You know I can't do that," the doctor called out from the overhead speakers. There was a coldness in his voice that enraged Lynch.

"Franklin, you piece of shit! Open this door right now!" he screamed with fury. Out of the corner of his eye he could see the dark wood ape headed his way. His gait was slow yet determined and there was hatred in his eyes.

Lynch continued to pull and work at the door handle, hopeful that Franklin was just toying with him and would unlock it remotely at any moment. The moment he hoped for never came. The wood ape bore down over him and grabbed him by the back of his skull. Lynch screamed out in pain as he was yanked backward and lifted off the ground by his head. The wood ape began chattering furiously at him, though Lynch had no clue what message he was trying to deliver. Lynch took his last breath and the wood ape's hand squeezed hard on his skull, bursting it like a grape.

CHAPTER 9

Doctor Franklin rubbed at his temples and tried desperately to fend off the headache that was brewing there. He'd just watched his best three guards get slaughtered by the wood apes he'd just released. Clearly, he'd underestimated the wretched creatures and now he was seeing the consequences of his actions. He now found himself in a situation that he himself could not contain alone. There were procedures and protocols on how to deal with situations such as these and Franklin had prided himself on the fact that he'd never had to resort to any of them in his almost two decades at Walker Laboratory. Now, things had taken a dramatic turn for the worst.

With a mixture of reluctance and shame, Walker pushed back from his desk and hurried down the hallway to the control room.

"Good afternoon, doc," a portly man said when he entered. The man had his feet up on the desk and was eating a sandwich. "Do we have our visitors in custody yet?"

"I need you to initiate protocol five," Franklin said, ignoring the question.

The man pulled his feet from the desk and put his sandwich aside. "What happened?" he asked.

"None of your concern at this time," Franklin replied. "Just do it now."

"Y—yessir," he said, and he immediately opened a panel next to him with a red T-handle implanted in the wall. He then grabbed the handle and turned it counter clockwise.

There was a rumbling under their feet, somewhat like the rumbling that had occurred when all the exterior windows and doors were sealed off.

"What do we do now?" the man asked, worry in his eyes.

"Now, I go make a phone call and we wait for help to arrive," Franklin said as he turned to leave the control room. He paused and glanced over his shoulder. "And relax…everything underground is now sealed off. No one can get out and no one can get in until we allow it. You're safe up here."

"What about all the other employees down there?" the man replied.

Franklin sighed and turned away. "If you pray, then pray for them," he said.

***

Chaos. That was the best word Sheriff Ray Cochran knew how to describe it. They'd found a door that led to another hallway and as soon as they'd stepped into it, the fluorescent lighting overhead flickered off and was replaced by red strobe lights that left them feeling a sense of looming dread. There were more lab workers that poured into the hallway with them, panic on their faces.

"Sheriff Cochran," one of the employees called out. "What are you doing down here? What is happening?"

It was a young woman, probably mid to late twenties. Her hair was curly, shoulder length and she wore black rimmed glasses.

"I have no idea what is happening," Cochran replied. "I was hoping one of you could tell us."

Another man in a white lab coat jogged up and grabbed the woman by the arm. "Julie let's go...we need to go hunker down in the cafeteria until this is over."

"And what exactly is *this*?" she asked, annoyed.

The man looked at her and then to Cochran. "Sheriff, what are you doing down here?"

"I think he's tired of getting asked that question," Marie snapped. "I have a question of my own. Where the hell is Kurt Bledsoe?"

The man and woman looked at each other and then back to her.

"You know he's here?" the woman asked, her eyes widening.

"Hell yeah I know he's here," she replied. "And just so you know, it's why he's here," she added, jerking a thumb toward the sheriff.

"Do you know where he is?" Cochran asked.

"Yes, of course," the woman answered. "I've been treating him." She suddenly seemed troubled.

Marie grabbed the woman's shirt and yanked her forward. "Where is he?" she asked through clenched teeth.

The man in the lab coat attempted to reach for Marie's arm but Sheriff Cochran stopped and put a hand on his chest to hold him back.

The woman looked down the hallway behind her. "If you take a right at the end of that hall, you'll find him in holding cell three."

Marie was taken aback. "He's in a holding cell?" she asked incredulously.

Before the woman could answer, a loud crash occurred behind them. Sheriff Cochran swung around and peered back toward the door that they'd just come out of. Something was on the other side of it, banging furiously.

"It's them!" Tony shouted.

The woman, apparently sensing what he was talking about, immediately looked to her male counterpart. "We need to go…now!"

"Shit," the man muttered anxiously. "I guess now we know why there is a lockdown."

The two of them ran away, disappearing around the corner at the end of the hallway. Once again Cochran, Marie, and Tony were all alone. The banging continued on the other side of the door.

"I told you they could open that hatch," Marie said, pulling her gun.

Sheriff Cochran pulled his own weapon again. "We need to get going," he said, the red strobe lights flashing across his stubbled face. "Let's get your brother and then get the hell out of here."

Cochran led the trio to the end of the corridor where they took a right as Julie had instructed. The lighting was dim, but the pulsating red lights provided enough illumination for them to see the signs over the various doors along the hallway. Each sign had a number on it, a black plate with white numerals.

"Number three," Marie said, pointing to a door on the left.

Sheriff Cochran grabbed the handle on the door to open it, but it stood firm.

"Of course, locked," he muttered in disgust.

There was a sudden crash from the hallway where they'd just come that made all three of them turn in a startle.

"They're through," Tony whispered. "They're coming..."

Cochran took a deep breath and grumbled something incoherent. He then struck the door in frustration and turned to Marie.

"We're gonna have to retreat and then come back when it's safe," he told her.

He could clearly see that she wanted to argue when he looked into her green eyes, but she reluctantly nodded. Cochran motioned for them to follow and they began to retreat further down the hallway. They'd passed at least six more cells when the worst thing Cochran could've imagined occurred. They hit a dead end.

"Shit," Marie spat, slapping the hollow block wall. "What now?"

Before the sheriff could respond, Tony gasped in terror. Cochran looked over at him and watched as he raised his arm and pointed back down the hallway. There were at least six large silhouettes moving in their direction. Slowly and methodically. The sheriff raised his gun and pointed it in their direction as Marie did the same.

"What do we do?" she asked worriedly.

"Hold your fire until I give the go ahead," Cochran replied. "I mean it, don't fire until I tell you."

She nodded but kept the barrel of her gun pointed aggressively toward the approaching wood apes. If the creatures could see the guns, the weapons did nothing to dissuade them.

"Tony," Cochran whispered. "Try the doors to these cells closest to us while we can still reach them."

Tony glared at him with disbelief. "You want me to move toward them?"

"We won't let them touch you...and the longer you wait the closer they're getting," Cochran shot back.

With great reluctance, Tony moved to the cell closest to him on the right side of the hallway. It was marked with the number nine but otherwise was identical to every other door they'd passed. He grabbed the handle and pushed with his shoulder. It did not budge.

"Try another...hurry!" Cochran urged.

Tony made a passing glance toward the wood apes that were still approaching and had no doubt that they could see him too. The flashing red strobe lights made their presence even more sinister, but he did his best to ignore it and keep focused on the task at hand. He hurriedly checked the door across the hall but got the same result.

"Grab that axe," Cochran said suddenly.

"What axe?" Tony asked, surprised.

"In the red cabinet beside the fire extinguisher…grab it now!"

Tony, finally realizing what the sheriff was referring to, pulled the glass door open and retrieved a fire axe from within the red cabinet. He then quickly retreated to stand beside Marie. "Wh— what am I supposed to do with this?" he stammered nervously.

"Get ready to use it," Cochran grumbled. He then paused and shot a quick glance to Marie. "Get ready…I think we're about to have to try to shoot our way outta here."

Marie nodded and gave a half smirk. If Cochran didn't know better, he'd have sworn she was excited about the prospect.

"Remember…not till I say," the sheriff reminded her, and she nodded again in response.

The wood apes continued to move slowly toward them and their foul stench began to fill Cochran's nostrils. His mind wandered a thousand directions as he frantically tried to come up with another solution that didn't involve emptying his weapon. He heard one of the creatures begin to chatter their strange language toward the others. It was then that the idea came to him.

"Marie, save your ammunition," Cochran said. "When I tell you both to run, you run like hell all the way to the other end of this hallway. Stay to the right side and against the wall and you'll be fine."

Marie looked at him incredulously. "Excuse me?" she asked. "How the hell do you think we'll be able to get by them?"

"Trust me," Cochran replied. "When I say go...you go. When you get down there I want you both to try every damn door you can until you find one that opens—and then I want you to get inside. I'll be right behind you."

Tony looked at Marie, clearly skeptical of the sheriff's plan, but he said nothing.

"Okay," Marie said, her own bit of skepticism dripping off the word. "When you say go...we'll go."

Cochran took a deep breath and aimed his gun with purpose. "Alright...GO!" he shouted, and at that same moment he pulled the trigger.

The bullet discharged from his gun hit its intended target and the red fire extinguisher that was on the wall exploded in a white cloud of nitrogen and chemicals. Marie and Tony did as they'd been instructed and stayed close to the wall, concealed within the white cloud, while the wood apes darted to the opposite side to escape the strange turn of events. Cochran hurried after them and began coughing violently as he mistakenly breathed some of the chemical into his lungs. Fortunately, Marie and Tony managed to avoid the same mistake and went to work on the doors at the far end of the hallway. To their amazement and relief, the first door they tried swung open, and the three of them plunged inside. Cochran, still suffering from a coughing fit, kicked the door closed with the heel of his boot and immediately locked it.

CHAPTER 10

They found themselves in a room with five lab technicians, two of whom were the man and woman that they'd met when they'd first stepped onto level four.

"This is because of you three, isn't it?" the dark-haired man asked, a hint of disgust in his voice.

Sheriff Cochran was still coughing, unable to respond, but Marie stepped forward and poked a finger in his chest. "I don't even know what *this* is," she snapped loudly. "All I do know is that my brother is being held here against his will and I want to take him home."

The woman that the man had called Julie spoke up, attempting to diffuse the tension. "I'm so sorry about the situation with your brother," she said, gently placing her hand on Marie's forearm. "Did you find his holding cell?"

"Yeah, we found it," Tony interjected. "We found it about the time those monsters you guys have been keeping down here broke in and came after us."

"We were forced to leave him," Marie said. "I'm not leaving without my brother, even if it means I have to kill every damn sasquatch walking around in this building."

The man chuckled, which drew a disapproving glance from Julie.

"Don't be an ass, John," she muttered with an eye roll.

"Well you know as well as I do that she won't be killing every monster in this building," he replied, still chuckling.

"And why the hell can't I?" Marie asked, her rage building.

John placed both hands on his hips, pulling back the edges of his lab coat slightly. "Well let's just say there's something else another level down that make these wood apes look like the puppets from *Sesame Street*."

Tony felt a chill run up his spine and he reacted with an obvious shiver. Marie noticed it but pretended not to.

"What's down there?" Sheriff Cochran asked, finally able to speak again.

Some of the other lab technicians had been listening and were visibly shaken by the topic of discussion. John noticed this and waved the sheriff off in an attempt to put the conversation to rest.

"No," Cochran said, stepping toward him. "Tell me what the hell is down there."

"I've already said too much," John answered.

"Tell me how to get out of here then," the sheriff snapped back.

John smiled. "There is no getting out of here until Franklin lets us out," he answered. "The building is on lockdown. The only other way to get these doors open right now is to turn off the generators and then cut the power."

Cochran perked up. "Okay great, then why don't we do that?"

John shook his head but said nothing.

"Because our test subjects could then escape," Julie explained.

"Umm…they've already escaped!" Marie said, dumbfounded.

"Some of them have," John said with a smirk.

Cochran was about to grab him by the collar of his coat when suddenly something slammed hard into the door. Marie pulled her gun and pointed it toward the door and Cochran did the same.

"Great," John said, annoyed. "You led them right to our hiding spot."

The door was struck again, and this time the metal jamb around it jarred.

"We gotta do something quick or they're coming in," Cochran said, still pointing his gun at the door.

For the first time, he took a moment to examine the room. Two of the walls were lined with metal cabinets, both high and low. Between them a metal countertop ran the length of the walls. There was a table in the middle and on the remaining walls there were doors. One of which they'd just entered through.

"What's behind that other door?" Cochran asked frantically.

"That's nothing more than a storage closet," John answered.

There was another loud crash and it sounded as if the door was getting ready to give. Cochran raced over to the storage closet, swinging the door open. It was a small space, probably six by six and it contained a couple of brooms, a mop and other cleaning materials within.

"We're running out of time," Marie shouted over her shoulder.

Cochran turned to face the lab employees. "You all have been working on these damn things...what can we do to stop them?"

"When we work with them they're under sedation," Julie said, sounding a bit panicked. "There isn't a whole lot that will stop them when they're in this state."

Tony moved toward the closet, dragging the fire axe behind him. When he peered inside, there was no secret hatch inside as he'd desperately hoped to find. What he did see, however, was a large air duct that ran across the ceiling with a grate that seemed to hold an air filter.

"What about getting out through here?" he asked, pointing up.

Cochran darted over to investigate and smiled as he saw the grate. He then looked over his shoulder, his eyes gazing the environment.

"Can we fit in there?" Marie asked, looking up.

"It's quite large," John answered. "There's a lot of air that has to be circulated down here. The ducts will have plenty of room and seem to be our only means of escape."

Cochran continued to look over the room and his eyes finally settled on a metal stool in the far corner. Quickly, he made a dash for the stool and then returned to the closet. There was yet another loud crash which in turn caused Tony to spin around and raise his axe in defense. The door held, but it was beginning to crack badly in the center.

Wasting no time, Cochran climbed onto the stool and quickly removed the grate and filter. There was a hole roughly two feet by two feet, providing just enough room for a human being to slip through.

"Let's go!" he shouted, jumping from the stool.

Without hesitation, John scrambled onto the stool and began to pull himself into the duct.

"Don't you think we should let the kid and the ladies go first?" Cochran asked him with disgust.

John didn't reply, only grunted as he pulled himself up to safety. Another lab technician approached but Cochran shoved him back.

"Let the kid up," he snapped, motioning for Tony to come forward.

Tony tossed the axe aside and shuffled into the duct, followed by Julie and then Marie. Two more lab technicians clambered up just as the door finally burst inward. The enraged wood apes poured in behind it. Sheriff Cochran made a motion to grab the remaining lab technician but was too late. The poor man was ripped backward, and the wood apes swarmed over him at once, pummeling and eventually tearing him apart. There were screams, but they were short-lived as the life of the man was extinguished quickly. Cochran slammed the door to the storage room shut and then scrambled up into the duct.

Once inside, he looked to his right and could see John, Julie, and the other lab technicians crawling away into the darkness. To his left, Marie and Tony sat, waiting.

"We're not going that way," Marie said. "Kurt is this way and this duct is our ticket into his cell."

Sheriff Cochran glanced over his shoulder once more at the darkness in the other direction. He knew that the lab technicians would know where a safe place to retreat would be. He also knew, however, that he'd come there to retrieve Kurt Bledsoe and that was just what he intended to do.

"Tony, maybe you should follow the others," he suggested.

Tony's brow furrowed, and he looked to Marie and then back to the sheriff.

"It's alright if you want to go with them," Marie said. "No one ever expected all of this to happen and I'd hate for something to happen to you."

Tony sighed and shook his head. "I'm staying with you," he told Marie.

"Alright…let's go," Cochran said, fully aware that there was no time to argue the matter further.

Marie pulled the flashlight she'd brought and then began crawling. She led them through multiple turns that made Cochran question whether she actually knew where she was going.

"Won't the wood apes come after us?" Tony asked. He was crawling between Marie and the sheriff.

"Not through here," Cochran replied. "They're much too big."

"That's good," Tony said, clearly relieved. "We should stay up here then."

"Do you know where you're going?" Cochran asked Marie, no longer able to keep quiet.

"No," she admitted. "But my gut tells me we're going the right way."

"Well that's comforting," Cochran replied, a bit of sarcasm in his tone.

They passed multiple vents, occasionally stopping to peer into the rooms below. Most of them looked like hospital rooms, empty except for a bed and a couple of chairs. After what seemed like fifteen minutes, Marie excitedly told them that she spotted movement. The three of them huddled around the vent and what came into focus was not what they were expecting. It was another wood ape and it seemed to be pacing back and forth in the room. The bed had been overturned as well as the chairs. There was other medical equipment tossed about, all of which now appeared to be destroyed.

"Well we certainly don't want to go in there," Tony whispered. "Let's keep looking."

He pulled back, expecting Marie to do the same, but she remained where she was. She continued to stare for a long time, saying nothing. Cochran for his part was staring intensely too. There was something different about this particular wood ape. It moved about the room differently and something about the way it carried itself made Cochran think its intelligence was a bit higher too. The creature continued to pace about the room and seemed to get more and more anxious with every step. Finally, it stopped, and to their horror, it peered up at the vent where they were watching it. The creature sniffed the air and approached the vent, keeping its eyes locked on them. It was then that Marie spoke up again.

"I don't believe it," she said, her voice just above a whisper. "I just can't believe it."

"Can't believe what?" Cochran replied, though he sensed he already knew the answer.

"That's Kurt...th—that's my brother."

CHAPTER 11

Before Sheriff Cochran could react, Marie managed to kick the vent off the duct and began to drop into the room in a fluid motion that seemed to take only a second.

"Wait," he called after her, and he literally hung out of the duct in an attempt to snatch her back.

Marie landed on the tile floor awkwardly, falling onto her side. The wood ape looked at her curiously and then lumbered toward her. She could only look up at it as the creature's large shadow loomed over her.

"Marie!" Cochran shouted. "Get back up here...now!"

If Marie heard him, she didn't show it. Her eyes were trained only on the beast standing over her.

"Kurt?" she said, her voice soft, yet steady.

The wood ape stared at her, cocking its head slightly. Its mouth opened, revealing rows of fangs that made her take a deep breath. After a moment, the creature knelt and began to sniff her hair. Marie looked up at Cochran and Tony, the both of them watching wide-eyed and seemingly overtaken with fear.

Marie reached up and gently touched the beast's face. "Kurt...it's me," she said. "It's Marie."

Moments after touching its face, the creature pulled back and let out an unsettling guttural growl. The sound was terrifying, and Marie pushed back from it, scrambling away until her back was against the wall. Overwhelmed with concern for her safety, Sheriff Cochran immediately pulled his gun and took aim. He initially took aim for the beast's head, but suddenly he caught sight of what Marie had seen as well. There was something far different about this wood ape's eyes when compared with those of the other beasts Cochran had encountered since they'd become trapped in the bowels of Walker Laboratory.

"What are you waiting for?" Tony asked suddenly.

The young man's voice startled the sheriff. Without giving the matter a lot more consideration, he moved the barrel of the gun toward the beast's left leg and fired. The report of the gun echoed loudly inside the confined metallic walls of the duct and the sheriff and Tony immediately closed their eyes as their ears began to ring.

"No!" Marie screamed as the wood ape howled loudly, a mixture of agony and pain.

It limped toward the metal door and began to beat both of its fists against it, desperate for an escape. Marie regained her footing and then looked around the room for something to aid her in getting back into the duct. As she surveyed her surroundings, her eye caught sight of the blood pouring from the wood ape's leg and she again thought of her brother. If the creature was indeed Kurt, the sight of the injury brought on concerns that were unavoidable.

With little regard for her own safety, she made her way to the terrified wood ape.

"What the hell are you doing?" Sheriff Cochran called out to her, just as his hearing was returning.

"He's hurt," she said, her eyes remaining on the beast.

"Yeah, he's hurt," Cochran replied. "I shot him before he could hurt you! Now get back over here."

Marie ignored the sheriff's pleas and drew closer to the beast she now believed was her brother. "Kurt," she said, gently placing a hand on the wood ape's shoulder.

It turned to look at her. There was no anger in its eyes, only a mixture of pain and fear. Once she was convinced it was not going to hurt her, she knelt slowly to examine the wounded leg. "I'm so sorry this happened," she said, glancing up at him. Her eyes then drifted to other parts of the room. She was searching for bandaging of any kind and when she found none, she grabbed the pillow off the hospital bed and yanked the case off it. Marie then quickly ripped it into strips of cloth that she then fashioned into a bandage around the beast's injury.

The wood ape looked down at what she'd done and then his green eyes met hers. Marie knew she was looking at a mirror image of her own and if there had been any doubt before that it was indeed Kurt, it was now gone completely. She didn't understand what had happened, of course, but she knew that if he was going to get any sort of help to overcome it, she had to get him out of that laboratory.

"Marie, get back here," Sheriff Cochran snapped at her as he dangled from the opening in the shaft. "We're not certain that's even Kurt."

She whirled around to look at him. "I'm certain that it *is* him," she snapped. "And I'm not going to leave him."

Cochran pulled back and sighed deeply. After a moment, he looked back down at her and said, "Okay, fine...we're going to make our way back into the hallway and find someone that can open that door. You sit tight."

She nodded and replied, "Please hurry."

"You're just going to leave her with that thing?" Tony asked in disbelief.

Cochran snorted and began crawling forward through the duct. "If it wanted to hurt her it would've done it by now," he said. "She's convinced it's Kurt."

"And what do you think?" Tony asked as he struggled to keep up.

"Kid, I don't know what to think anymore," the sheriff grumbled.

Sometime later they finally came upon a grated vent that revealed a hallway underneath them. Sheriff Cochran wasted no time kicking the grate free and then hanging out of the opening to investigate, his gun drawn. There were more flashing red lights, but otherwise the dim corridor was empty. The two of them dropped down onto the white tile floor and cautiously made their way forward. It took him a moment to get his bearings, but

Cochran soon realized they were in the same hallway that they had entered after escaping the room full of wood apes.

"So, what do we do now?" Tony asked, panting slightly from the excitement and physical exertion.

Sheriff Cochran ignored him for a moment as his eyes darted around in all directions searching for danger. "Well we already know that the doors ain't opening until we find a way to cut the power. There's got to be a maintenance closet somewhere where the generators are at. We find those generators, we cut the power, then we get Marie, Kurt and ourselves the hell out of this house of horrors."

Tony nodded but there was concern etched on his face. "What about what the guy said earlier...about letting out other test subjects?" he asked nervously.

Cochran shook his head and waved off the comment. "Once we get Marie and Kurt out of that room, we're not going to wait around long enough to find out what else is lurking down here."

CHAPTER 12

Sheriff Cochran knew that the quickest way to find out where the generators were located, was to find someone that worked in the lab that could point them in the right direction. He returned to the room where the wood apes had broken the door down and forced them, and some of the lab workers, to escape through the network of air ducts that ran above the ceiling. He remembered that John, Julie, and some of the other lab employees had gone the opposite direction from the route he, Marie, and Tony had taken. He tried to work out in his head which way the air ducts would've taken them, and he began to move down another hallway whilst staring at the ceiling, Tony in tow.

"Do you know where you're going?" Tony asked.

"No clue," the sheriff replied. "But we've got to figure out where the others went so we can find out where the maintenance rooms are at."

Tony stayed close, occasionally glancing over his shoulder to see if they were being pursued. There were multiple times that he thought he could hear movement behind them and at any moment he would not have been surprised to see the wood apes bearing down on them. After a while they came upon a door with a large window that had chicken wire embedded within the panes of glass.

The words **COOL STORAGE** was spelled across the glass in black vinyl lettering. Beyond the window there were rows of what appeared to be large refrigerators adorning stainless steel doors. They covered the entire back wall, top to bottom. In front of the refrigerators, there were two lab employees huddled together on the floor. It was John and Julie; the two Walker Laboratory associates they'd met earlier.

Cochran rapped on the glass with his knuckles, which in turn immediately startled them.

"Let us in," he said to them, though he figured they wouldn't be able to hear his voice.

Julie and John looked at each other and were speaking. Cochran sensed they were debating on whether to let him in. It was then that Cochran noticed something else. There was quite a bit of blood spatter on Julie's face and even more blood on the front of her white lab coat. As the two of them continued to have a discussion, the sheriff heard movement somewhere around a far corner of the hallway. The flashing red lights produced terrifying shadows of multiple wood apes moving around, seemingly approaching Cochran's position.

He returned his attention to the occupants of the room and again beat his knuckles on the glass. Julie looked over at him, her eyes sad and tired. With great reluctance, John stood and made his way to the door. He unlocked it and the sheriff and Tony barged in.

"Took you long enough," Cochran grumbled as he locked the door.

"If it were entirely up to me, I wouldn't have opened it," John quipped as he returned to where he'd been sitting next to Julie.

Cochran glanced at Julie and she refused to look back. He again took note of the blood spatter and redness in her eyes—a suggestion that she'd been crying.

"What happened?" he asked, looking back to John.

John huffed and kept an arm around Julie. "What the hell do you think happened?" he asked angrily.

"The guys that were with you...they're all dead?" the sheriff asked.

John nodded but said nothing. Tony shuddered and moved to a far corner as if it would somehow provide a minimal amount of protection.

"Has anything like this ever happened before?" Cochran asked.

John shrugged, still saying nothing.

"We've had subjects escape from their cells before," Julie said suddenly, her voice a bit raspy. "But never this many at one time. It's too many and we're going to be picked off one by one unless someone does something—and fast."

Sheriff Cochran drew near her and knelt on one knee. "So, help me do something about it," he muttered.

She looked over at him, her eyes filled with hopelessness. "How?" she asked.

Cochran took a deep breath and rubbed at the back of his neck. "For starters, tell me what the hell has happened to Kurt Bledsoe?"

Julie looked to John and he responded by shaking his head.

"We can't talk about it," he said to her.

Cochran's brow furrowed, and he resisted the urge to punch John. He instead reached down and took Julie by the hand, squeezing slightly.

"Listen," he said softly. "I can get us out of here, but I'm not leaving without what I came here for—and that is Kurt. I need to know what's happened to him."

Julie shifted uneasily, and John kept his eyes locked onto hers. After a long moment, she pulled away from him and stood. She walked over to a mirrored supply cabinet mounted on the opposite wall and looked into it.

"We were aware of the substance that leaked from the meteor—it's something we've encountered before," she said, still staring at herself.

John suddenly stood. "Julie, keep quiet," he growled. "You're not at liberty—"

"Oh, shut the hell up John," she snapped at him, exasperation in her tone. "If you haven't noticed, we're probably all going to die down here so who gives a shit at this point if we tell them the truth."

John opened his mouth to speak again, but Sheriff Cochran marched toward him. "You keep quiet," he grumbled, pointing at him.

John opened his mouth again.

"I mean it," Cochran said. "Keep your mouth shut or I'll shut it for you."

John sighed and then put his hands into the pockets of his lab coat. He kept quiet.

"Go on," Cochran said. "Tell me everything."

She turned to look at him, her expression made it seem as if her train of thought suddenly took her a different direction. She leaned against the wall beside the mirrored cabinet and said, "Sheriff, this county is inhabited by Bigfoot...are you aware of that?"

Cochran nodded. "Yes, I've known of their presence for quite some time."

Tony suddenly spoke up. "Wait...what?" he asked, surprised. "You've known these things live around here?"

"Yes," he replied. "But that's not important right now...go on, Julie."

"I thought you may know about them," Julie replied. "With your role in law enforcement...how could you *not* know about them?"

Cochran placed his hands in the pockets of his jacket and paced for a minute. "I know there is a tribe of them out there," he said. "And although there are other residents in this county that have seen them too, the general perception has hovered around them being a mythical presence and nothing more."

Julie smiled slightly and cocked her head. "I'm sure there are a lot of people in this county that would disagree with that sentiment," she said.

He looked at her, his eyes widening. "Well, it's what I'd like to believe anyway," he conceded.

She reached up and removed her glasses, seemingly noticing for the first time that there was blood spatter on the right lens. She cleaned it with the tail of her shirt. "Are you aware of some of the other strange occurrences that go on in this county?" she asked, still focused on the glasses.

The sheriff took a deep breath and released it slowly. "I've heard lots of things," he said. "But I don't believe what I don't see with my own eyes."

Julie put her glasses back on and then crossed her arms. "Well I'm here to tell you that whatever you've heard…it's probably true."

She stared at him intently for a moment and he stared right back.

"What are you saying?"

"I'm saying that Baker County Mississippi has been a hotbed for supernatural activity for quite some time. No one knows why exactly but given that fact the United States government has taken a great interest in the area as you can imagine," she explained. "It's why this laboratory was put here."

"So, we're talking about aliens now?" Cochran asked, arching an eyebrow.

Julie's mouth remained a straight line. It was as if she'd finally decided she'd said enough.

"Oh, you're done now?" Cochran asked, annoyed. "Okay, fine...but I still want an explanation for what has happened to Kurt."

Julie looked over at John. "Tell him what you know," she said.

John was sweating and appeared clearly uncomfortable with the conversation that was taking place. His body language seemed to suggest more than anything he could've said that he wanted the topic of discussion to go another direction. At first, he kept his mouth shut and looked away. Julie cleared her throat and shot him an icy glare that apparently changed his mind.

"The substance that leaked from the meteor...it's biological," he said, his voice trembling a bit. "It's a living thing—like a parasite."

Sheriff Cochran shifted his feet and scratched his head. "So, you're saying this stuff transformed him?"

John shook his head. "Not exactly," he answered. "The Gallium—that's what we call it—is notorious for taking more than one host at the same time. It has a way of merging two organisms together into one being—or three, I suppose if you count the Gallium."

Tony stepped out of the corner, his curiosity getting the better of him. "Kurt's body has merged with a Bigfoot?" he asked.

John nodded. "That's correct."

"For what purpose?" Cochran asked. "I mean, why the hell would this Gallium stuff you're talking about want to merge two species together?"

"It feeds on them and will eventually kill them both," Julie answered. "That's why our work with Kurt is so important. We're trying to find a way to remove the Gallium before it's too late."

"So, if you get it out of him, will he return to normal?" Tony asked.

John shook his head. "I'm afraid it doesn't work that way," he answered. "If we're able to get the Gallium out of his system, the merging of his body with the Bigfoot is irreversible. He'll have to share that body from now on if he survives."

Sheriff Cochran cursed under his breath and chewed his lip as he digested the troubling news he'd just heard. "That's ludicrous," he murmured finally. "You're telling me there's nothing you can do to get him back to normal?"

John shrugged. "As of right now...no."

"And what about the wood ape he's sharing a body with?" Cochran asked. "Is it controlling things, or is Kurt? How does all that work?"

"Oh, the Bigfoot is very much aware of what is going on just as Kurt is," Julie said. "And you must understand that there is still a lot that we are learning, but there are obvious behavioral and personality shifts that have occurred frequently since Kurt was brought here. It's very obvious to us that he is not always the one in control."

"So, what happens when the wood ape is in control?" Cochran asked, though he was worried about what the answer would be.

John stepped toward him, his hands on his hips. "Very primal," he answered. "A lot of thrashing, and gnashing of teeth. It looks at us with a hatred I've never seen before and I have no doubt that when it gets that way, if it wasn't restrained it would no doubt rip whatever human is in front of it limb from limb."

Sheriff Cochran's heart rate suddenly increased, and he looked over at Tony as they both immediately became overwhelmed with the same concern.

Marie.

CHAPTER 13

"I'm so sorry this happened to you," Marie said again.

It had been at least the fifth time she'd said it, but there was nothing else fitting of the situation she could think of to say. The creature that she knew was her brother stared at her, his green eyes sad and confused. They were seated on the tile floor, their backs against the wall. Marie had placed her hand into his now large, callused and weathered palm.

"Don't worry," she said soothingly. "The sheriff and Tony are gonna get this door open and we're gonna get you out of here. We'll find someone that can help you and get you fixed right up."

Kurt kept his eyes on her and his expression suggested he was unconvinced. He breathed deeply, his large lungs causing his chest to noticeably rise and fall with every breath. Marie attempted to get up to stretch as her legs were aching fiercely. Kurt pulled on her arm to keep her down beside him. She could see the fear in his face, although it was a strange sight considering the size and power he now possessed in his new frame.

"I'm not going anywhere," she said. "Just need to stretch my legs."

With obvious reluctance, Kurt let her go. He watched her stretch and then pace the room a few times. It was then that he felt it. The sensation was subtle at first, but he was beginning to become quite accustomed to it and he certainly now knew what it meant.

The beast is coming, he thought.

***

"Do you want to live or not?" Cochran asked, his tone a bit scathing.

"Yes," Julie responded. "But I want you to understand what is going to happen if you go through with this."

"How can I understand it when you won't tell me what I need to know?" he snapped back. "Whatever it is you're hiding down here can't possibly be any worse than what's already loose."

"That's where you're dead wrong, Sheriff," John said. He then marched over to Julie and grabbed her by the forearm. She looked at where he'd clutched her arm and then her eyes met his. "You tell them how to cut that power off, we're dead and you know it."

She wrenched her arm free. "As we've already discussed," she replied angrily, "I think we're dead either way so what damn difference does it make?"

"It makes a difference because if we can hold out a bit longer, the cavalry will be here—you know Franklin has called them."

Julie lowered her head a bit and then looked over at the sheriff. "He's right about that," she said. "Help is on the way."

Cochran shook his head and placed his hands on his hips, pushing the bottom sides of his unzipped jacket back slightly.

"How do you know that?" he asked. "I mean really…how do you know that for certain? How do you know Franklin hasn't already tucked tail and left this place?"

Julie's eyes narrowed, and he could see that she was mulling the possibility over.

"He's not doing that," John said, seemingly reading her thoughts.

"John, the best I can tell, everyone else down here is already dead," she replied. "We're all that's left. The doors that will grant us freedom will not open unless someone up there opens them, or we figure out a way to open them ourselves."

"There is no reason to open the doors right now," he replied, almost pleadingly.

Sheriff Cochran had finally had enough. Without hesitation, he pulled his gun and pointed it at John. "I'm a little tired of you constantly standing between me and my way out of here. Now Kurt is currently with his sister and they're locked in a cell together. From what you've told me, he is essentially a ticking time bomb and can switch over to Bigfoot mode at any time. I don't have time to listen to your excuses any longer. Tell me where the maintenance closet is so that I can cut the power."

John clenched his teeth and glanced over at Julie. She nodded at him, urging him to give the sheriff the information he'd requested.

He sighed and muttered a curse word under his breath. "Alright," he said, sounding defeated. "You've got to go down another level. There's a red line painted on the floor of the hallways. Follow that line and it'll take you to the maintenance area you're looking for."

Cochran pulled the gun back and returned it to the holster on his belt. He then turned toward the door. "Tony, let's go," he said.

"Right behind you," Tony replied.

"Wait!" Julie called out behind them.

Cochran glanced back over his shoulder at her.

"Go left, there is a stairwell at the end of the hallway. If you go right, you'll probably run into trouble again," she said.

"Thanks," he said. "I suppose you don't want to join us?"

Julie took a step forward, but then glanced over at John. He was shaking his head.

"No," she said a bit reluctantly. "We'll be able to tell when the power goes down completely, and when it does, we'll get out of here."

The sheriff frowned and glanced over at John. "If anything happens to her, it's on you," he said, pointing at him. "Y'all sit tight until the power goes down…and when it does, make a beeline for the stairs and get the hell out of this building."

"We will," Julie assured him.

There was a moment of hesitation as Cochran felt a deep desire to plead with her to follow him, however he resisted the urge to follow his instinct. Without another word, he and Tony entered the hallway amid the eerie shower of red light and the increasingly loud stench of the nearby wood apes.

***

"What the hell is taking them so long?" Marie asked as she paced between the walls of Kurt's cell.

It seemed the longer she had been in there, the smaller the room became. She looked at her watch and estimated at least half an hour had passed. A passing glance at the open vent in the ceiling caused her to briefly consider leaving the cell and trying to figure out how to open the door on her own. Marie couldn't help but wonder if maybe the sheriff and Tony had been caught—or worse yet, killed. She shuddered at that thought and refused to accept it.

Kurt, meanwhile, had become quite lethargic and distant. At first, it seemed obvious that he recognized Marie and knew who she was. Furthermore, he seemed to understand that she, the sheriff, and Tony were all working together to try and free him. Though he could not talk, his eyes said a great deal. Now, however, the liveliness that had been Kurt Bledsoe seemed to be fading into something…else.

"Are you okay?" she asked, kneeling beside him.

Kurt stared straight ahead, emotionless though his eyes began to turn a darker shade than what they'd once been. A bit of drool fell from the corner of his mouth and his large hands rested on the floor beside him, palms up. Marie began to feel a bit uneasy, so much so that she regained her footing and moved to the opposite side of the room, just watching him.

After a period of several minutes the creature that had once been Kurt finally turned its large head and peered over at her. The eyes had finally settled on a dark shade of brown and the beast's head cocked to the side, clearly confused and curious about what was going on. Marie looked on as it clumsily stood, using the sturdy wall to support the enormous frame.

"Kurt?" she asked, though she seemed quite aware that he was no longer there.

The wood ape glared at her and then responded with a low guttural growl. Marie felt her heart rate increase and tried desperately to remain calm.

"Kurt, it's me," she said softly. "It's Marie. I need you to focus…to hear my voice."

The wood ape took a step toward her, still growling. It was a hulking beast with wide shoulders and a muscular build. She took note that it was larger than all the other wood apes she'd encountered in the laboratory. The creature took another step and at that point Marie did something she really did not want to do.

"Stop right there," she said firmly. The barrel of the gun she was pointing at the wood ape shook slightly, but she kept it steady enough to do the job if it came to it.

The creature looked at the gun and then down to the bandaged wound on its leg. It seemed to know that the two were connected, and it did nothing but fuel the already mounting frustration.

"Please don't make me use this," Marie said pleadingly. "Kurt, I know you're in there...please don't make me use this. Stop where you are now!"

The creature *did* stop, but whether Kurt was behind it, she could not be sure. Marie's back was against the wall, there was no where else to go, but up into the air ducts again if it came to that. Even then, she didn't know if she'd be able to do it before the wood ape grabbed her.

Sheriff Cochran...please hurry, she thought.

CHAPTER 14

"Keep up...and stay close!" Cochran commanded as they entered the stairwell.

Tony did as he was told, though he was fearful enough to do it anyway. They reached a door and it was apparently the final level. The door was labeled CONTAINMENT LEVEL 5. Sheriff Cochran opened it carefully and peered into the hallway. There was no one there, and no movement at all except for more flashing red lights on the ceiling. He glanced at the floor and immediately saw the red line that John had mentioned—the line that would lead him to the power source.

Cochran pulled his gun again and motioned for Tony to follow as he scrambled into the hallway. As they moved along the corridor, he noticed more labs on either side, and through the windows he could see more lab workers hiding within them. The employees looked terrified and watched them curiously as they continued to follow the red line. None of them made a move to open the door.

"Do you see those people?" Tony whispered.

"I see them," the sheriff replied. "We don't have time to check on them right now. Let's find the power and get back to Marie before it's too late. I'm sure she's wondering where the hell we've gone off to."

After a series of twists and turns through the hallways, finally they encountered the door they'd been looking for. Cochran barged in, pushing the door open so hard that it crashed into the wall as it swung around. There were multiple large generators humming in front of them, all of which were elevated on a massive concrete platform.

"How do we turn them off?" Tony asked.

Cochran climbed some metal steps that led to a large control panel. There were multiple knobs and switches. After looking it over a moment he found what he was looking for. He turned to Tony and tossed him his flashlight.

"Get ready to turn this on," he said. "It's about to get real dark."

Tony nodded as Cochran turned back and grabbed the large switch labelled MAIN POWER. Without hesitation he flipped it off and at once the flashing red lights ceased. They instantly became enveloped in pitch black darkness. A second later, the flashlight Tony was holding flickered to life.

"Give me the light back," Cochran said. "Stay close to me...we've got to move fast."

They stepped back into the hallway and began following the red line again to find their way back to where they'd first entered level five. They'd been travelling only a minute when a piercing shriek unlike anything they'd ever heard echoed from somewhere up ahead. It was a nightmarish sound and Cochran felt the hair on the back of his neck stand on end.

"What was that?" Tony asked.

Sheriff Cochran had stopped dead in his tracks and listened intensely. The shrieking happened again. It was both haunting and otherworldly—unlike anything he'd ever heard before. And then…the screaming started.

"Oh my god…oh my god," Tony began to mutter over and over.

Cochran pointed the beam of the flashlight ahead of them and kept the gun tight in his other hand. "We've got to keep moving," he said, his voice just above a whisper. "Obviously, something else has gotten free—and it ain't no wood ape. Stay close and stay quiet."

Tony nodded and hurried after the sheriff as soon as he began moving. They walked briskly, staying just fast enough to keep a good pace, but slow enough to stay quiet. When they drew near the windowed laboratories where the employees were hiding, Cochran slowed his gait dramatically. There was no sound there anymore and he wondered if the screams they'd heard had originated from those very rooms. With great reluctance, he shined the beam of his light into the windows and immediately got his answer.

Tony dropped to his knees and wretched. Cochran turned to tell him to be quiet but realized the boy could do little to help it. The scene before them was horrifying, and nothing a teenage boy should have to see. The door to the room had been broken loose from its hinges. The windows were mostly painted red with human blood and chunks of flesh. The lab workers, or what was left of them, were sprawled awkwardly all over the room. The chest cavities of each had been torn open, and it appeared to Cochran that each of the corpses' hearts had been removed.

"Get up," he said, glancing over at Tony. "We've got to keep moving or we'll end up like them."

"What in the hell did that? And where did it go?" he replied, still fighting the urge to throw up.

"I'm not sure I want to find out the answers to either of those questions, Tony," Cochran answered. He held out his hand to pull him up. "Come on…keep moving."

Tony nodded, and seconds later they were off again. As Sheriff Cochran began to climb the stairs to return to level four, for the first time he began to feel the pains of exhaustion. It seemed that ever since he'd entered Walker Laboratory hours earlier, he'd been not only running for his own life, but trying to keep Marie and Tony alive as well. He was desperately hoping that the end of the terrible day was now near its end since all the doors should now be unlocked, ultimately providing their ticket to freedom. His main concern now, however, was the well-being of Marie. She'd been in that cell with Kurt for a very long time.

Upon reaching the entry to level four, Cochran paused and put the side of his head against the door.

"What are you doing?" Tony asked curiously.

"Listening, now keep quiet," he snapped in reply.

After he was satisfied that it was safe, he slowly turned the handle and opened the door. The hallway was much like what they'd left on level five, total darkness. There were no sounds, good or bad. Cautiously, Cochran moved into the hallway with Tony tight on his heels. They stayed close to the wall and did not stop until they reached the cell where they'd left Kurt and Marie. To Cochran's surprise, the door was already opened, and when he shined the flashlight inside, he was dismayed to find it empty.

"Maybe she's already made a run for it," Tony said.

Cochran looked over his shoulder at him. Even in the darkness he could see how terrified the young man had become. Truthfully, Cochran couldn't help but feel proud of how brave he'd been through the entire ordeal. Exhaustion, both mental and physical, had to begin taking its toll on him too.

"It's possible," the sheriff replied. "But we've got to be sure. I brought her here and I need to make sure she got out."

"What are you saying?" Tony asked, clearly uneasy with the answer he'd gotten.

"Don't worry," Cochran said. "We'll be out of here very soon. Now, keep up with me."

The sheriff turned back into the hallway and began the brisk walk deeper into the bowels of level four. He decided the first place he'd check was the room where he'd left John and Julie. Though the responsibility he felt for them was far less than that of Marie and Tony, there was a responsibility his job bound him to, nevertheless. As they approached the doorway, the beam of the flashlight shone across a glossy dark surface on the tile floor ahead. It was clearly blood—and a lot of it.

Cochran stopped in his tracks and considered turning back. He knew at least one of them had to be dead, there was just too much blood for the outcome to be any better. When he thought of the wood apes and the mystery creature that had escaped on level five, if he and Tony continued onward their odds of survival would continue to diminish. Cochran could live with continuing to put himself in harms way, however putting Tony in further danger was getting harder for him to justify.

"Sheriff Cochran," a feminine voice suddenly whispered from somewhere inside the room. It was a familiar voice...it was Marie's voice.

Cochran quickly stepped through the slick pool of blood and into the room, his gun and flashlight still leading the way.

"Marie," he said. "Is that you?"

"Yes, get in here and get down," she replied.

Cochran crouched down and followed the sound of her voice, the beam of his light finally finding her sitting in a corner between two lockers. Next to her was Julie, her eyes reddened and puffy. Cochran made his way over and plopped down in front of them.

"Are you two alright?" he asked, his voice as low as he could get it.

Marie nodded but Julie was unresponsive. She just kept her head down.

"Where is John?" he asked.

Marie sighed and glanced over at Julie who immediately began to sob.

"Oh no," Cochran said.

Marie's expression was all the confirmation he needed. "That's his blood in the doorway," she whispered somberly.

"Dammit," the sheriff replied in disgust. "What got him?"

It was at this point that Marie began to cry. "Kurt...Kurt got him," she replied.

Tony crawled closer to where they were talking. "What?" he asked. "We left you with Kurt. If he didn't attack you then why—"

"He changed," Marie interrupted as she wiped the tears away from her eyes, smearing mascara as she did so. "At first, he was fine, and I felt completely safe with him, but then..."

"Then what?" Cochran asked, leaning closer. "What happened?"

"H-he changed," she replied. "His eyes changed...his whole damn personality changed. Suddenly, he wasn't himself anymore."

Sheriff Cochran reached over and grabbed Julie's forearm. "Honey, did you tell her what you told us?" he asked.

"Tell me what?" Marie asked, looking over at her.

Julie shook her head. "No," she muttered just above a whisper. "I didn't get a chance. The thing chased her in here and John tried to intervene. It didn't end well."

The sheriff looked over his shoulder. "Where the hell is he now?"

Marie shook her head. "I don't know, he dragged John out of here and disappeared down the hallway. He will probably be back."

"Which is why we need to move," Cochran replied. "I assume you two are okay...you can walk?"

"I'm not going anywhere without my brother," Marie shot back, her words firm.

Cochran sighed and closed his eyes. "Marie, you said yourself that he's not himself anymore. I'm thinking maybe you should start to consider that the Kurt you knew is gone for good."

She frowned, and her eyes tightened as she tried desperately to fight off more tears. "I can't accept that," she said, her voice trembling. "He's all I have left."

Suddenly, Tony moved closer and held her hand. "Marie, he's the best friend I've ever had," he said softly. "And I don't want to give up any more than you do. So, tell me...at what point do we give up?" he asked.

She glared at him, her expression a mixture of confusion and anger. "What are you trying to say?" she asked.

"I'm saying," he continued, "that I don't want it to take Kurt tearing you apart and killing you for you to finally come to the realization that he's gone."

Her green eyes locked on his and he could see that she suddenly understood what he was trying to say. She took a deep breath and then nodded slowly. "Alright," she said, closing her eyes. "Let's get out of here before it's too late."

Cochran smiled and patted her leg. "Atta girl," he said, rising to his feet. He offered a hand and pulled her up while Tony did the same for Julie. "I promise you, I'll tell you what I know when we get out of here," he said, and then he glanced over at Julie. She looked away, seemingly ashamed of her role in the ordeal.

Once all of them were on their feet again, they turned to make their exit. What was in front of them stopped them immediately in their tracks. Julie and Tony gasped at the exact same time while Cochran and Marie immediately pulled their guns. Looming in front of them stood the six wood apes they'd been trying to avoid for hours now. The dark one, the largest and seemingly the leader of the pack, snarled and released a nightmarish roar that rattled all their bones.

CHAPTER 15

"What do we do?" Marie asked, her voice quaking.

Out of the corner of his eye, Sheriff Cochran could see the barrel of her gun shaking. "Hold that thing steady," he muttered back to her. "Stay calm!"

"Sorry, but that ain't gonna happen right now," she replied.

The massive dark wood ape took a step toward him and then the others moved too, though none of them dared step past him.

"This is it…we're going to die," Julie said, and she began to sob again.

"We can't give up…we can't give up," Tony said—and he said it again, and again.

"Okay, here's what we're gonna do," Cochran said as sweat trickled down the front of his face. "I'm going to open fire and do everything in my power to make them all come after me. And when I do, you three get your asses out of here."

Marie glanced over at him in awe. "Are you out of your mind? That's a terrible idea!"

"Well it's all I've got," he snapped back. "If you've got a better one, I'm all ears."

"There has to be something we can do that doesn't require you to get killed," she answered.

"Again, I'm open for suggestions," he said.

The dark wood ape drew even closer, but it eyed the guns Cochran and Marie were holding with intense curiosity. Each step seemed to be calculated and made with a healthy dose of caution.

"No more time," the sheriff said. "On the count of three…"

"No," Marie said. "I said no."

"You don't get a vote," Cochran replied. "One…"

"Dammit, don't do this…there has to be another way!"

"Don't think so. Two…"

"Please," she pleaded. "Don't do this!"

Cochran took a deep breath, closed his eyes and said the word. "Three!" he said, as he simultaneously pulled the trigger. "RUN!" he thundered.

They did run, amid the sound of a barrage of bullets as the sheriff unloaded his gun into the chest of the dark one that was towering over him. With tears in her eyes, Marie made a beeline for the door. She assumed the others were behind her. The wood apes that had not been shot seemed to be overtaken with fear and confusion. Marie thought, as crazy as it was, that the sheriff's plan just might work. She was nearly to the door when a flash of something gray darted through the opening, bumping into her just hard enough to send her sailing against the wall. She howled in pain as something in her left shoulder popped.

"What was that?" Tony asked, as clearly he'd seen whatever had zipped into the room too.

There was no opportunity for anyone to answer. At that very moment whatever had entered the room began tearing into the five remaining wood apes. Sheriff Cochran had stumbled backwards as he emptied the magazine in his handgun. He'd landed on his bottom and then frantically reached for another magazine. He was struggling to find it and had just about accepted he was going to die when the horrific scene began to unfold in front of him.

At first, he was unable to see anything, but he could hear plenty. Something large, and swift was moving from one wood ape to another, viciously tearing into them with teeth, or claws or both. He could hear the splatter of blood and what he thought could be the breaking of bones. The wood apes that were dying barely had enough time to emit a yelp before they were cruelly executed in some sort of otherworldly fashion.

Cochran retrieved his flashlight and quickly shined the beam on to the carnage in front of him. What he saw was horrifying and made his jaw drop. The creature stood as high as the wood apes— at least eight feet in height. The skin covering its body was a deep gray and completely hairless. The head was large and round, as was the black bulbous eyes on the face. There were two slits for a nose and the mouth opened to reveal a frightening maw of needle-like teeth which at present were all stained red with blood. The body was humanoid in appearance and there were no clothes on the creature's back. As if the face was not frightening enough, it was the hands and claws that had truly rattled him.

Each hand comprised of five digits, much like a human hand. What was unlike a human hand, however, were the jagged claws protruding from each finger. There was blood and tissue dangling from the claws and the sheriff began to understand that these were the instruments of death that he'd heard ripping into the wood apes.

He'd only had a second to take in the creature's nightmarish features before the thing moved onto the next wood ape. With his mouth agape, the sheriff looked on as the creature thrust its clawed hand forcefully into the chest of its next victim and in the blink of an eye it had retracted the hand with a bloody heart clutched in the palm.

Cochran resisted the urge to scream in horror as the creature quickly tossed the heart into its mouth as if it were feasting on nothing more than a piece of popcorn chicken. The thing went on to continue the same act until all the wood apes in the room were no longer living. Cochran looked around at the corpses surrounding him and then his gaze slowly moved to the gray being breathing heavily in the center of the room.

"It's alien," Julie called out from a darkened corner. "It's the monster you kept asking about."

Cochran didn't reply. He instead began to fumble around in search of the other magazine for his handgun. The creature watched him curiously as it continued to breathe heavily. Cochran finally found the magazine, but his hand was shaking so violently he struggled mightily to get it into the gun.

Just when he'd nearly gotten it, the alien hissed at him loudly, startling him so badly that he dropped it. The magazine clanged loudly on the tile floor and the sound seemed to anger the alien as it hissed again loudly in response.

"You three get out of here," he said, his voice trembling. "What are you waiting on? This is your chance to get out of here!"

The alien began walking toward him, its clawed feet slapping hard against the tile as it walked. It seemed to be taking its time which was a stark difference from how it had handled the five wood apes minutes earlier.

"I mean it," Cochran called out. "You three get out of here. Don't watch this!"

The alien had finally stopped a mere two feet away from him. Cochran slowly moved the beam of his light up the creature's legs and abdomen, finally settling on the terrifying face. Its mouth opened slightly, and a silver strand of saliva hung from the lower row of teeth. The alien then reached down and snatched Cochran off the floor by the collar of his shirt. The sheriff closed his eyes and waited for his heart to be ripped out. He prayed it would be quick and painless.

Suddenly, a thunderous boom rang out from the opposite side of the room and a bullet tore through the alien's abdomen. The creature hissed and shrieked loudly. Cochran whipped his head around and could barely make out Marie standing to the right, the gun in her hand smoking slightly.

"Keep firing!" he yelled.

She did, and every single bullet tore through the creature's body. Its blood appeared to be black—as black as its eyes. Abruptly, Cochran was dropped to the floor and the wounded alien zipped across the room to dispose of Marie.

"No!" Cochran screamed out. "Come for me you son of a bitch!"

If the alien heard his pleas, they were ignored. The creature thrust its arm forward, the dagger-like claws leading like the tip of a spear. Marie screamed as she knew what was coming.

CHAPTER 16

When the alien's claws stopped in mid-air, Marie guessed there could not have been more than of inch of space between them and the skin over her heart. The alien hissed loudly in anger as it glared over at the beast that had grabbed its arm and prevented the killing blow. There was a large hairy hand around the alien's forearm. Marie followed her savior's arm up until she met the creature's eyes. Even in the darkness she could see that they were green.

"Kurt!" she shouted jubilantly.

The alien immediately turned its attention to the wood ape that was Kurt Bledsoe and the two of them then engaged in a fierce battle to the death. The alien, now wounded by the multiple gunshot wounds it had taken, was no longer able to move as swiftly as it was used to. Despite its wounds, the creature was still fiercely strong. It grabbed Kurt by his right arm and leg and swung him through the air like a frisbee. He sailed through the air, crashing through a large pane of glass and finally stopping after contacting the wall on the opposite side of the hallway.

The alien jumped through the broken window and attempted to thrust its claws into Kurt's chest, but he was ready for the attack. The clawed hand was caught again in the same fashion that Kurt had caught it to save Marie's life. This time, however, Kurt used the power of his new body to bend the alien's wrist backward, breaking it with a sickening *crack*. The alien shrieked in pain and instinctively thrust its free hand forward to pierce Kurt's abdomen from the side. Kurt sensed the attack and moved slightly, avoiding a killing blow, but he was unfortunately unable to avoid the alien's claws altogether. They instead raked across his side, penetrating deep enough to contact his ribs. Kurt howled in agony and then thrust his other hand forward to grab the alien by the throat.

The alien attempted to remove Kurt's grip from its throat with its good hand. It used its claws to try and rip the hairy hand around its neck to ribbons, but to no avail. It seemed the harder it clawed at the hand, the harder Kurt squeezed. The act went on for at least a solid minute before the creature's black eyes bulged and then its body went limp. With the alien dead, Kurt collapsed to the ground. His right hand was bleeding profusely.

Marie quickly moved to his side to examine the hand. "Kurt," she said as she knelt beside him. "I knew you were still in there...I knew it!"

Kurt looked over at her, his green eyes shimmering. If Marie didn't know better, she'd have sworn that he smiled slightly.

"I need something to wrap his hand!" she called out.

Tony suddenly emerged from the darkness, dropping beside her. "Here," he said, handing her a white towel.

She went to work wrapping the hand and applying pressure. Julie then appeared and had a roll of medical tape in her hand.

"Found this in one of the drawers," she muttered. "Keep the towel over the wounds and I'll wrap it tight with tape."

Marie nodded and the two women went to work with what they had. Once they'd finished, Marie looked at all the blood on her hands and the floor.

"He's lost a lot," she said worriedly.

"Not enough to be worried about," Julie replied. "As long as that bandage holds, and he doesn't lose more."

Suddenly Kurt reached over with his good hand, placing it lightly over Marie's. She looked at him, her eyes welling with tears. "I'm going to get you out of here," she said. "I don't know how, but I am."

"They'll never let him leave this building alive," Tony said, disheartened.

"Who is *they*?" Cochran said suddenly from the shadows. "Franklin?"

"That's exactly who I mean," Tony replied. "I'm sure they'll be waiting for us on the ground level."

Marie shook her head. "No," she said angrily. "Not when we're this close. Sheriff, we've got to get him out of here!"

"If we're going to do it, it'll take all of us, and we'll have to move now," he replied. "If the government is involved you can bet there will be lots of soldiers with firepower arriving if they haven't made it here already."

"I'm in," Julie said. "I feel some responsibility for what has happened here. I want to help get him out."

"Good," Cochran said, he then glanced to Tony and Marie, shining the light on both of them.

"What do you need us to do?" Marie asked.

"First," Cochran replied. "We need more firepower."

"And where do you suggest we get it?" Marie replied, and she looked to Julie. "My best guess would be that any guns in this building would be found upstairs somewhere."

Julie considered the question, and then her eyes lit up as something occurred to her. "Three guards were killed on level three," she said. "I heard about it from one of the other employees. The wood apes killed them, and they were armed with handguns."

"Perfect," Cochran said. "Get Kurt up and let's move!"

Julie and Marie both worked together to get Kurt on his feet. They then all followed behind Cochran, who led the way with the flashlight, to the stairwell and eventually on to level three. Upon entering the cell where the vicious wood apes had once been contained, the sheriff immediately noticed the gory remains of Lynch and his counterparts.

"Wait out here," he commanded, not wanting the others to see the grisly scene. He quickly collected the guns and made his way back into the hallway.

"Okay," he said, handing a gun to both Julie and Tony. "Here's the plan. Marie and I will lead the way when we get to the ground floor. We're going to quickly make our way out of the front door, but if we encounter anyone along the way, no one uses these weapons unless I say so…got it?"

"There's no way it's going to be that easy," Tony said as he stared at the gun. "I don't even know how to use this thing."

Marie snatched it from him and turned off the safety. "All you've got to do, is point it and pull the trigger," she explained. "Don't point it at anything that you don't intend to kill."

"Right," Cochran said. "Keep that thing pointed at the ground unless we get into a situation where I tell you to use it. As far as it being easy…no, it's not going to be easy," he admitted. "It's gonna take a lot of luck, and I'll say this: If the National Guard is already out there, all bets are off. We surrender."

Marie glared at him, somewhat surprised.

"I'm sorry honey," he replied. "But that's the best I can do. I'm not going to get you all killed."

"So, let's say we get outside, then what?" Tony asked. "Kurt isn't fitting in your car!"

Cochran sighed as he realized he hadn't thought that far ahead. It was true. In his new form, Kurt was much too large to fit in his patrol car.

"I've got a pickup truck," Julie said suddenly.

They all looked at her simultaneously and Cochran smiled. "As I said, we'll need a little luck," he replied. "So, we'll use Julie's truck to get him out of here and then we meet up at the old Dunn Cemetery on the outskirts of town."

He glanced up at the ailing creature that had once been Kurt Bledsoe. He looked weak and exhausted. The blood loss seemed to be taking a toll on him. And then he noticed something else.

His eyes seemed to be darkening and no longer seemed as green as they once had been.

CHAPTER 17

When they reached the ground floor, Sheriff Cochran was pleasantly surprised to see that there was no longer a need for his flashlight. The beige hallway and white tile floor were lit up nicely by the usual fluorescent lighting and he was pleased to be free of any flashing red strobe lights. They moved along the corridor as quickly and as quietly as possible. It was quiet—eerily quiet, so much so that Cochran couldn't help but feel a sense of impending dread.

They rounded a corner that would lead them to the lobby and their eventual freedom but were stopped dead in their tracks by the appearance of Dr. Franklin and two armed guards standing in their way.

Franklin eyed them carefully and then allowed a smile to creep across his face. "I've got to hand it to you," he said. "I never dreamed you'd be able to make it out of there alive."

"Are you saying you were actively trying to kill us?" Cochran asked, his eyes narrowed.

Franklin huffed and showed his teeth. "I can't let you leave this building, especially with *that*," he added, pointing to Kurt.

"Just what are you going to do to stop us?" Cochran asked, raising his gun. Marie did the same.

The guards flanking Franklin responded by raising their own firearms.

"Okay, slow down," the doctor said, a hint of worry in his tone. "No need for there to be any more blood shed than what has already occurred."

"I agree," Cochran replied. "So, get the hell out of our way."

Franklin opened his mouth to respond, but before he could, Kurt unexpectedly collapsed to the floor behind Tony. Marie whipped around and dropped down to the floor beside him.

"Kurt!" she said anxiously. "Kurt, open your eyes. What's wrong?"

Franklin shook his head with a look of forced empathy. "Can't you see he's succumbed to his injuries?" he asked. "The best place for him to be is here. If you care anything about his well-being, you'll step aside and let us tend to him."

Marie gently patted Kurt's face, and then looked up at Franklin. "Absolutely not," she hissed. "You stay the hell away from my brother!"

Sheriff Cochran felt his heart sink when he realized that Kurt had collapsed to the floor. He kept his gun pointed forward but barely noticed the armed security guards moving closer to him. He seemed to be frozen, and unsure of what to do.

If Kurt is dead, all is lost, he thought. *What would be the point in keeping this going? No one needs to die...*

Slowly, reluctantly, Cochran lowered his weapon.

"Drop them on the ground," Franklin ordered.

The guards moved past the sheriff as he did indeed drop his gun to the floor.

"What are you doing?" Marie called out when she noticed what he'd done. "Why are you giving up?"

"It's over Marie," he said, defeated. "Tony, Julie, do as he says and drop your guns."

"No!" Marie screamed, but it was to no avail. Their guns clattered to the ground and they stepped aside as the guards moved to where Marie and Kurt were on the floor.

For a moment, Marie considered fighting them—after all, she still had her gun. When she glanced at Kurt's eyes, however, she noticed something quite troubling. It was something she'd noticed before when they'd been locked in his cell together. The green color had dissipated and been replaced with a dark brown that was almost black. She knew at that moment that Kurt had, at least temporarily, checked out. Marie dropped her weapon to the floor and stood.

"All four of you step over here," Franklin said, motioning for them to step toward the lobby. "I assure you, you've made the right decision. Let my men take Kurt back downstairs where they can resume—"

Suddenly, without any warning at all, the wood ape that shared a body with Kurt Bledsoe sprang to life. It grabbed the guard closest to him by the throat and twisted its wrist, resulting in a sickening *cracking* sound of breaking bones in the man's neck. The guard's lifeless body dropped to the floor and then the wood ape turned its attention on the other man. He managed to fire off one shot that hit the creature in the shoulder, however it did nothing to slow him down. The wood ape grabbed the guard's right arm around the bicep and jerked hard, ripping the appendage from the rest of the man's body. The guard screamed in agony as a shower of red blood sprayed wildly from the gaping wound. In mere seconds, the guard passed out from the pain and blood loss, dropping to the tile floor next to his dead counterpart.

Sheriff Cochran shouted for Julie and Tony to exit the building and get to his car. They wasted no time doing as they were told and rushed past him, too shocked to speak or scream. Cochran then turned his attention to Marie. She was just standing there watching as the wood ape killed the two guards right before her eyes. There would be no reasoning with her, he knew, so he did the only thing he could think to do in the moment. Cochran rushed to her from behind and grabbed her around the waist. She screamed and fought at him as she realized he was trying to physically remove her from the building. Hard as she tried, Cochran was too strong. There was no way she could wrench free of his grasp.

Dr. Franklin, seemingly mesmerized by what he'd seen, stepped toward the wood ape that shared a body with Kurt. He, however, did not seem to be aware that the two entities alternated control of the body.

"Kurt," he said, his tone soothing and pleasant. "This is Dr. Franklin...do you remember me?"

The wood ape glared at him with a mixture of hatred and curiosity. It cocked its head slightly and its brow furrowed. As Sheriff Cochran made his way through the exit of Walker Laboratory, Marie's screams rang out loudly in his ears. They weren't loud enough, however, to drown out the pitiful screaming of Dr. Franklin as he was torn apart limb from limb.

***

The National Guard *did* show up almost half an hour after Sheriff Cochran, Julie, Tony and Marie escaped Walker Laboratory. Cochran, not really knowing where else to go in the moment, drove his patrol car straight to the station where he was greeted by a very distraught and worried Shelly.

"Sheriff Cochran! Where on earth have you been?" she asked, almost scolding him.

"Long story," he'd replied when he made his way inside. "Get me a number to the governor."

Shelly was taken aback. Her usually rosy face turned ashen. "Oh my...the governor?"

"You heard me," he said as he flipped on the lights to his office.

Tony, Julie, and a still sobbing Marie moved into the office, all taking a seat. Shelly looked them all over, and then stared at the sheriff.

"Shelly, I'll explain later," he replied, trying to sound patient. "But now, I *really* need you to get the governor's office on the phone."

She nodded and retreated to the front desk to make the call. Just as she sat down, a black car with dark tinted windows came to a screeching stop in front of the building.

"Sheriff Cochran," Shelly called out worriedly. "We've got a visitor up here!"

Cochran jogged out of his office just as two men and one woman entered the front door. The men were dressed in black suits with dark sunglasses. The woman was dressed similarly but in a pants suit, and no sunglasses. The man in front removed his sunglasses and held out his hand as he met Cochran in the foyer.

"Sheriff Ray Cochran, I presume," he said as the sheriff took his hand and shook it.

"That's me," he replied, arching an eyebrow. "Can I help you?"

The man chuckled and glanced over his shoulder at the woman to his left. "Sheriff, there's no need for us to skirt around what's been going on for the past several hours is there?"

Cochran sighed but said nothing. The man appeared friendly, but as he well knew, looks could be deceiving.

"Listen," the man said, leaning in a little closer. "There's no need to be alarmed. You're a member of law enforcement, so that grants you a bit of..." he paused as he searched for the right words.

"A bit of, professional courtesy," he said finally. "What I'm more concerned about at this point is Tony Joyner and Marie Bledsoe."

Cochran felt his mouth drop open. "How the hell do you know their names?" he asked, surprised.

"Can we trust you to keep them quiet as well?" the man asked, ignoring his question.

Cochran scratched his head. "What do you mean?" he asked, genuinely confused. "You want us to keep quiet about what happened over there at Walker Laboratory?"

"That's *exactly* what I mean," the man replied. "You all must keep quiet or I'm afraid the department I work for can and will make each one of you go away. What you saw in that laboratory must never be discussed with anyone. I realize what happened to Marie's brother was a terrible tragedy, but she must move past it now." He paused, and his mouth tightened as the expression on his face grew darker. "Sheriff, you must keep her quiet or she will disappear. Do you understand what I'm saying?"

Cochran nodded slowly. "I understand," he said. "We will not discuss what happened there with anyone. I just want them to be left alone."

The man smiled and returned the sunglasses to his face. "And they will be," he replied. "As long as they—and yourself of course—keep your mouths shut, nothing further will ever come of this—er, incident. My department will clean up this mess like it never happened."

"And what happens to Kurt Bledsoe?" the sheriff asked, though something inside him screamed at him not to.

The man leaned close again and lowered his voice to a whisper. "Well," he muttered. "You didn't hear it from me, but he escaped the building before my people got there. Must have gotten out right after you."

Cochran's eyes widened as the man pulled back from him again.

"But again, you didn't hear it from me," the man repeated. "Now," he said, seemingly changing gears. "What are all of you gonna do when I walk out of this door?"

The sheriff stared at him but said nothing.

The man rolled his eyes behind the dark glasses. "Sheriff, I need to hear you say it," he said. "Tell me what you and the others are gonna do when I leave here."

Cochran licked his lips and then said, "We're not going to speak about what happened at Walker today."

The man smiled widely. "That's it," he said. "That's what I was looking for." He turned to walk away but stopped once more. "Oh, and these two agents with me are John Milk and Emma Honeycutt. They'll be sticking around town for a while to make sure you follow through with your promise—and to investigate a few other strange occurrences in your county. Do me a favor and make sure they're treated well while they're here?"

Sheriff Cochran nodded.

"Thanks," the man said, and he pushed the door open.

"Wait," Cochran called after him.

The man glanced over his shoulder to look back at him. "Yes, sheriff?"

"What's your name?"

"Cornelius Cold," the man replied. "Very pleased to make your acquaintance, sir."

With that, Cold left the building with Milk and Honeycutt in tow. They returned to their vehicle and left just as quickly as they'd arrived. Shelly, who'd been watching the entire exchange from behind her desk, slowly stood and moved near the sheriff.

"Sheriff Cochran," she said gently. "Do you still want me to call the governor?"

He shook his head. "No, I don't think it'll be necessary now," he replied, as he turned away to go and have a hard discussion with Tony, Julie and Marie.

"Okay, but can you please tell me what this is all about?" Shelly called after him.

Sheriff Cochran paused in the doorway of his office and looked over at her. "Sorry Shelly, but you heard the man. I'm to never speak of what happened last night again."

THE END

CHECK OUT OTHER GREAT CRYPTID NOVELS

BIGFOOT WAR
by Eric S. Brown

Now a feature film from Origin Releasing. For the first time ever, all three core books of the Bigfoot War series have been collected into a single tome of Sasquatch Apocalypse horror. Remastered and reedited this book chronicles the original war between man and beast from the initial battles in Babblecreek through the apocalypse to the wastelands of a dark future world where Sasquatch reigns supreme and mankind struggles to survive. If you think you've experienced Bigfoot Horror before, think again. Bigfoot War sets the bar for the genre and will leave you praying that you never have to go into the woods again.

CRYPTID ZOO
by Gerry Griffiths

As a child, rare and unusual animals, especially cryptid creatures, always fascinated Carter Wilde.

Now that he's an eccentric billionaire and runs the largest conglomerate of high-tech companies all over the world, he can finally achieve his wildest dream of building the most incredible theme park ever conceived on the planet...CRYPTID ZOO.

Even though there have been apparent problems with the project, Wilde still decides to send some of his marketing employees and their families on a forced vacation to assess the theme park in preparation for Opening Day.

Nick Wells and his family are some of those chosen and are about to embark on what will become the most terror-filled weekend of their lives—praying they survive.

STEP RIGHT UP AND GET YOUR FREE PASS...

TO CRYPTID ZOO

CHECK OUT OTHER GREAT CRYPTID NOVELS

SWAMP MONSTER MASSACRE
by **Hunter Shea**

The swamp belongs to them. Humans are only prey. Deep in the overgrown swamps of Florida, where humans rarely dare to enter, lives a race of creatures long thought to be only the stuff of legend. They walk upright but are stronger, taller and more brutal than any man. And when a small boat of tourists, held captive by a fleeing criminal, accidentally kills one of the swamp dwellers' young, the creatures are filled with a terrifyingly human emotion—a merciless lust for vengeance that will paint the trees red with blood.

TERROR MOUNTAIN
by **Gerry Griffiths**

When Marcus Pike inherits his grandfather's farm and moves his family out to the country, he has no idea there's an unholy terror running rampant about the mountainous farming community. Sheriff Avery Anderson has seen the heinous carnage and the mutilated bodies. He's also seen the giant footprints left in the snow—Bigfoot tracks. Meanwhile, Cole Wagner, and his wife, Kate, are prospecting their gold claim farther up the valley, unaware of the impending dangers lurking in the woods as an early winter storm sets in. Soon the snowy countryside will run red with blood on TERROR MOUNTAIN.

CHECK OUT OTHER GREAT BIGFOOT NOVELS

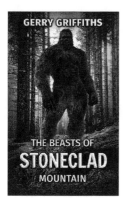

THE BEASTS OF STONECLAD MOUNTAIN
by Gerry Griffiths

Clay Morgan is overjoyed when he is offered a place to live in a remote wilderness at the base of a notorious mountain. Locals say there are Bigfoot living high up in the dense mountainous forest. Clay is skeptic at first and thinks it's nothing more than tall tales.

But soon Clay becomes a believer when giant creatures invade his new home and snatch his baby boy, Casey.

Now, Clay and his wife, Mia, must rescue their son with the help of Clay's uncle and his dog, a journey up the foreboding mountain that will take them into an unimaginable world...straight into hell!

BIGFOOT AWAKENED
by Alex Laybourne

A weekend away with friends was supposed to be fun. One last chance for Jamie to blow off some steam before she leaves for college, but when the group make a wrong turn, fun is the last thing they find.

From the moment they pass through a small rural town they are being hunted by whatever abominations live in the woods.

Yet, as the beasts attack and the truth is revealed, they learn that despite everything, man still remains the most terrifying evil of them all.

Printed in Great Britain
by Amazon

79122460R00087